I've spent most of my career in television drama. No screenwriter has ever written the heart-breaking drama that unfolds in an African slum every hour. I know. Thanks to Larry Jones and Feed The Children, I've been there. Through these pages, you will go too.

—SUSAN LUCCI
TELEVISION ACTRESS, *ALL MY CHILDREN*

Many American women possess phobic fear of sexual dominance by force. One thing could be worse: sexual dominance by force in the teeming underworld of an African slum. This book will enrich your life through fear, an unusual blend that's most effective when it works. In these pages, it does.

—KELLY MONACO
ACTRESS AND WINNER OF
DANCING WITH THE STARS, SEASON 1

Inside Kibera, an African slum, I personally staged a real-life rescue of an abandoned baby, and placed it inside Feed The Children's Abandoned Baby Center. I was blessed to spare one of millions of outcasts. This book will change your life, and eliminate any indifference you might have had toward human agony.

—MONTEL WILLIAMS
EMMY AWARD-WINNING TELEVISION
TALK SHOW HOST

This story packages the horror of a nightmare with the encouragement of an inspirational tome. Rarely has that been done. Brilliant!

—ERIK ESTRADA
TELEVISION AND FILM STAR

I have had the privilege of traveling to Africa with Feed The Children. I have spoken to the people and seen the conditions of this continent firsthand, and *The Virgin Cure* is a vivid reminder that throughout time, perhaps nothing has been more detrimental to the human condition than misinformation and superstition. This book validates that terrifying reality. It's truly a must-read page-turner.

—JERIOUS NORWOOD
ATLANTA FALCONS RUNNING BACK, NFL

I have seen the difference Larry Jones makes in the lives of the people of Africa while I was there with Feed The Children. He has spent many years and countless hours bettering the lives of so many. Larry has seen firsthand the unimaginable hardships the people of Africa have endured. His book, *The Virgin Cure*, is a riveting novel that will enlighten your mind, stir your emotions, and place your conscience exactly where it should be.

—DAVID WESLEY
RETIRED NBA PLAYER

LARRY JONES

CREATION
HOUSE
A STRANG COMPANY

The Virgin Cure by Larry Jones
Published by Creation House
A Strang Company
600 Rinehart Road
Lake Mary, Florida 32746
www.strangbookgroup.com

All Scripture quotations are from the King James Version
of the Bible.

Design Director: Bill Johnson
Cover design by Bill Johnson

Library of Congress Control Number: 2009935577
International Standard Book Number: 978-1-59979-942-1

First Edition

09 10 11 12 13 — 9 8 7 6 5 4 3 2 1
Printed in the United States of America

Preface

AJENE JABARI HAD always been an unwilling dreamer. Yet the visions that lit up his mind nearly every night were as much a part of his slumber as closing his eyes. So vivid were his dreams that he'd awaken in the morning with the distinct impression he hadn't slept at all. Exhausted, he sought out a sleep disorder clinic in the hope that he could find a way to curb this nocturnal onslaught. There, technicians attached electronic sensors to monitor his rapid eye movement, or REM cycle, the deepest part of sleep.

Test results showed that his sleep was as sound as

it was easy. So for Ajene, his dreams, while disturbing to him, were not interfering with the amount or the quality of his rest.

This was not good news for someone who longed for sleep without dreams, particularly those he found prophetic. Too often, his dreams told the truth. Too often, he disliked what they said.

Chapter One

C LICHÉS IRRITATED AJENE Jabari. He considered people who peppered their speech with them to be incapable of original thought.

His own children knew better than to use "the more the merrier" when pleading their case for having their friends over to spend the night. His boys could look forward to a sharp reprimand should they declare, "No pain, no gain," when they exercised. As for "look before you leap," well, that was just idiotic. No thinking person, Ajene insisted, would leap anywhere without providing for a landing.

He blamed these tired, trite expressions on mindless American television, broadcast on several stations in Nairobi, Kenya, his beloved birthplace. He'd never been a fan of much of anything originating from the United States.

Ajene believed that his stance against unoriginal thinking had expanded his children's communication skills. They were all among the top of their class in language arts. And surely, the credit belonged to him; he was, after all, raising his children on his own.

On this afternoon at home alone, he was leisurely

flipping through a family photograph album. "A picture is worth a thousand words," he mused idly. He had no sooner said it than he was seized with disgust. What a hypocrite! Considering his campaign against hackneyed expressions, he was shocked he had actually used one that had been around probably since the advent of cave drawings. He was glad his three kids hadn't heard him; they would have teased him relentlessly.

But Ajene's thoughts did not stop there. *What is it about clichés? Why do they endure?* Then it occurred to him that their longevity is rooted in kernels of truth. "You can't win 'em all," "Beauty is only skin deep," "His bark is worse than his bite"—Ajene had heard these and others a thousand times, but only now did he really think about how true they were. For now, while perusing sentimental photographs, he was fixating on "Time flies while you're having fun."

Page by page, time replayed month by month within snapshots seen through Ajene's moistening eyes. Each image triggered a flashback of all the happy moments the camera had captured in the three years since he had adopted his three children. Ajene's kids would be home from school soon, but his trip down memory lane had made him miss them now. Though he wished they were by his side, it was probably good they weren't.

They'd think he was sad.

They were too young to understand happy tears, just

as they were too young to grasp why someone would wake up screaming, as he so often did. No matter. Deep in their own blissful dreamworld, his children were oblivious to their father's night terrors. Ajene was always quick to pull a pillow to his face to muffle his cries when a nightmare jolted him to wakefulness. And then he lay there, staring in mute terror into the impenetrable blackness of his room, his mind reeling from what his dreams had told him.

Memory is the lens that refocuses life's most vivid experiences. One can close his eyes to tragedy as it unfolds before him, but he can never truly close his mind's eye to unwanted recollections. For Ajene, memories were bullies. They ambushed him, pummeled him, and left him invisibly bleeding whenever they wanted.

"Most men lead lives of quiet desperation," he reminded himself, again forgetting his embargo against clichés.

Maybe, just maybe, he could endure the onslaught of recollection by simply going to sleep. Perhaps he'd get a head start on the hellish nocturnal parade, still several hours away. So he tried.

In the middle of the day, he closed his eyes and rested his head against the spongy cushion of the sofa. He felt safe. If the memories came, and if they were mean, he could simply open his eyes and the spectra would evaporate. Sunlight around him and photographs on his lap would thwart what the black, empty nights could not.

As his sagging eyelids ushered daylight into the gloaming, Ajene discovered something else about unwanted memories. They don't ease into one's mind—they bolt, like recollections in reverse.

Asleep, his dreams took him instantly to Kibera, the seething slum that some Africans called the blackest part of their dark continent. In sleep, he relived his entry into that infernal world.

> *As a member of Nairobi's privileged class, Ajene is teeing off on the lush fairway of a golf course near the presidential palace. The ball veers off and lands on the other side of the wall that separates this posh world from Kibera's unspeakable blight.*
>
> *His stubborn efforts to retrieve his errant ball take him through a bizarre series of events. His quest inside the dangerous slum eventually leads him to Moses, now his oldest adopted child.*

Suspended in the stage between dreaming and wakefulness, Ajene struggled in vain to bring himself into the light of consciousness. He fought to open his eyes, but his lids felt as heavy as wooden shingles. The dream beckoned him, and he resisted it with all his might because he knew what was coming next: his perilous escape with Moses, along with Kamau and Nyah, Moses's brother and sister.

>*Ajene sprints through the dim alleyways, with Kamau and Nyah in his arms and Moses at his heels. The darkness is pierced only by the blazing fire he'd started to divert murderous men chasing the children and him.*
>
>*Ajene hears the shouts of the knife-wielding pursuers who know Ajene has money—and that they never will. Blades drawn, they seek to even the score. He hears the panicked shrieks of Kiberans, whose flimsy cardboard huts are engulfed in flames.*

Even in sleep, he felt guilt, wondering whether any lives were lost inside the inferno he'd intentionally ignited to save himself. On his couch, he again smelled the stench of the small, fetid stream fouled by human and animal excrement that winds through Kibera.

>*In a desperate attempt to save their village, Kiberans dip into the rancid flow and throw handfuls of water on the blaze. The drips do little more than hiss. Panicked, some tear down the single shed Ajene had ignited rather*

than see its flames spread to another, then another.

Many people were badly burned, Ajene knew. He had heard their screams that night. He heard them again today.

Even as the sleeping Ajene relived the horror of that night, part of him knew he was dreaming, and he wanted out. His mind, racing to escape, turned away from the chaos to something familiar, something he could control: numbers.

From the shadows, a row of blurry numbers emerged. He forced his dozing mind to read it. So many zeros. Finally, he made it out: 1,000,000—the number of sick and dying crammed into Kibera's 550 acres. Another number flashed through his mind, 30. This one had haunted him since he learned it was the life expectancy of a person dwelling in the crime-ridden shantytown.[1]

The effort of focusing on the figures allowed him to escape the terrifying personal involvement in the Kibera alleyway. As his mind shifted, so did his point of view. Now in the dream, he floated above the scene and watched the action as a spectator.

He sees himself running from the angry mob, weaving through the crowds of people pouring into Kibera's alleys to investigate the hysterical shouts of "Fire!" People stagger from their huts and stare at Ajene in his expensive, color-coordinated clothes and gold wrist-watch, carrying two children in his arms and with another in tow.

Someone in the dream yells, "Baby thief!" Ajene looks back repeatedly on the mob behind him. Each time, their numbers are multiplied, much like the multi-headed Hydra of Greek mythology: every time the hero Hercules severed a head, two more grew in its place.

Now vicious dogs join in the chase. Ajene dodges one and leaps over two more. Another one lunges at him, teeth bared, aiming for Ajene's throat. He dodges—just in time, but he shudders imagining the cur's vise-like clamp on him.

Suddenly, a loud boom jarred Ajene awake. The dogs, the angry mob, and the fire were gone in the flutter of an eye. He was at home, safe, where he'd been all along. The heavy photograph album had tumbled from his lap and lay on the hardwood floor. Its impact had awakened him where he sat, breathing heavily and sweating lightly onto the sofa cushions.

But there was another noise. Was he still dreaming? No, this was in the real world.

Ajene bolted upright, trying to shake off the cobwebs

of his nap. He needed to be alert—now. The cavernous ceiling echoed with a noise he couldn't identify, a soft clanking sound.

The instant Ajene discerned it as key turning in the lock, the front door to Ajene's sprawling house burst open and in ran Moses, Kamau, and Nyah, their faces silhouetted by bright sunlight behind them. Their laughter filled the room, chasing away the last vestiges of sleep like a splash of cold water to the face. His children were home from school.

For what he really had and where he really was, Ajene thanked his real God.

This was no dream.

Chapter Two

AJENE RUSTLED TO his feet and told his children they'd caught him napping. He felt himself shiver and realized he'd been perspiring while sleeping deeply. The air conditioner had given him a chill.

His six-year-old son, Kamau, asked his dad if he'd been standing in the "indoor rain," the nickname his children had given the bathroom shower. They had never seen any kind of indoor plumbing before Ajene single-handedly brought them out of Kibera three years ago. The shower fascinated them—activating "rainfall" inside the house with the turn of a dial. "Indoor rain" became a family joke.

Ajene laughed a lot with his children, especially Kamau, who had been only three when he was carried through the fire during their escape from Kibera. He seemed to bear no emotional scars; indeed, he didn't seem to remember the treacherous ordeal at all. Nyah, now seven, was four when she was rescued. Like her younger brother, she had no idea Ajene had set their

house ablaze that fateful night in order to distract the
would-be killers who were about to take his life.

Moses, now ten, had remarkably overcome the
trauma from the terrifying ordeal. He'd grown into
a tall and stout child, having recovered entirely from
the malnutrition that plagued his early life when his
only regular meal was a lunch of porridge at a Kiberan
school. On weekends, he'd eaten only the greens bought
with income he earned by picking up discarded plastic
bags at a Nairobi dump. He was paid three shillings
per pound of plastic he collected. When he was seven,
he found out that his mother was dying of AIDS. What
he didn't know was that she'd contracted it by working
as a prostitute, desperate to feed him and his siblings.
Moses remembered her life of suffering, especially
poignant during her final days, when she explained
that he would soon have to become the provider for
the household.

After that, he carried the weight of the world on his
scrawny shoulders. His recollection of those hellish
times was now fading, thankfully. None of his friends
knew of his earlier life. His dark secret was known only
to his adoptive father. But neither ever mentioned it.

Ajene was amazed at how well Moses had defused
all of those unpleasant memories. Looking at his children's faces sometimes brought it all back to him. These
youngsters had experienced a miracle. Someday they

would realize it. For now, Ajene simply wanted them to be happy and carefree—as every child should be.

Months ago, Ajene had established "time to talk," a period when each family member, including him, shared stories about what each had learned during the day, and anything else of interest. For this, they convened in the kitchen every day after school.

The adoptive father decided he wouldn't speak this afternoon. He didn't want to share the images inspired by his troubled dream.

Claims of "me first" and "you were first yesterday" usually kicked off the sessions. Childhood rivalry lifted the spirits of the house and the formerly lonely man who occupied it. During the family's treacherous escape from Kibera, Ajene had almost died to give these children a new life. He often wondered who'd really given life to whom.

The novice father moved the trio into the kitchen, where no one had to tell them about cookies and milk. He did, however, have to scold Kamau when he sneaked a bite out of his sister's snack before easing it back onto her plate. The act prompted a scolding for Nyah, too, before she put pepper into Kamau's milk.

Though Ajene had never been married, he took to his role as stepfather as easily as these orphans had taken to him. People said these children had changed his life. He took them at their word. He could hardly remember what life was like before these siblings burst into it.

Someone once asked if fatherhood was the hardest job he'd ever loved. Thinking on the query, he realized he'd never previously loved at all.

Today's family summit began as each child started to recall the school day. The subject quickly turned to bragging on grades. Kamau and Nyah had garnered As on spelling tests. They chided Moses, who'd earned a lowly B on his test in African history.

The younger children charged that Moses hadn't studied hard enough. Pointing a finger accusingly, Moses insisted that their noise last night had interfered with his concentration. He told his dad that, at age ten, he was the most grownup child by three years. He therefore thought he had more in common with grownups than kids and asked if he could share a bedroom with Ajene. That way, the two could share "man talk" and not be distracted by a little brother and, even worse, a sister.

Ajene said he would consider the request and get back to Moses in about eight years.

The father silently thanked God for the way these youngsters had evolved into typical children. Their interactions consisted of the usual kid stuff: favorite and not-so-favorite classroom subjects, squabbling, and competing at everything they did.

What could be more normal?

They locked each other out of their rooms, argued about whose turn it was to load the dishwasher, vowed not to speak to each other ever again, and began each morning with no thought for the spats of the previous day. They woke up in a new world every day, just as children should.

They'd been together through hunger, unspeakable poverty, and the death of their mother.

Three years ago, each was depleted and listless, lying on the floor of a filthy hut. Their interests then were mutual—awaiting the day's leftover porridge that Moses brought from school. Weekends were worse. Then the wait for their next meal stretched on for two days.

But all that was behind them now. Nyah wanted to be a princess someday, Kamau wanted to catch a live frog, and Moses dreamed of eventually being in the Olympics as the world's fastest runner from the nation that had historically produced them—Kenya.

Suddenly Nyah jumped up, waving her hand in front of her nose and shouting that both her brothers stunk and needed showers. In the same breath, she insisted it was her turn to talk. Ajene wondered what relevance one contention had to the other. Meanwhile, Nyah kept bobbing up and down, holding her nose. Each boy muttered that it was the other who needed to wash.

Ajene turned his head to chuckle in personal delight.

"Go ahead, Nyah," he announced. "It's your turn to talk."

The boys got up and went to the sink, scraping crumbs off their plates, boldly demonstrating their disinterest in anything their sister had to say. Ajene pointed out that she had listened to them; therefore, they were courtesy-bound to listen to her. Kamau consented, but on one condition: that she didn't talk again about her desire for a Hannah Montana lunch box.

He and Moses agreed that Nyah only wanted the trendy brand because the other girls had one and because it came from America. Ajene responded that it didn't matter if it came from next door. It was Nyah's turn to talk.

He had learned about children from on-the-job training. He knew he could demand a stop to all the squabbling. But why would he? The children needed to learn how to live with each other's differences. Besides, he was always delighted to share their simple problems. All this might seem like sound and fury to them, but to Ajene it was the music of involvement and happiness.

At times, Ajene felt so overcome with joy that he was moved to tears. Nyah asked if he was crying because he felt sorry for somebody. He replied that he felt sorry for anyone who didn't have the love they shared together.

She said she didn't understand. Ajene said, "You will someday."

"We agreed it was Nyah's turn to talk. You boys listen to your sister," Ajene insisted with mock sternness in his tone.

"Yeah!" Nyah chimed, letting the room fall silent before she took the floor. "Guess where I'm going!"

The brothers rolled their eyes. Neither ventured a guess.

"OK, give up?" Nyah continued, responding to their silence.

More silence.

"I'm going on a field trip," she said, "with my whole class."

"You're taking a trip to a field?" Kamau asked. "Whose field? Are there frogs there?"

"A field trip," Ajene interjected, "is when a class of students visits a place they've never been before. Everyone learns about the people and other things in that unfamiliar place."

"That's right, I think," said Nyah, now jumping up and down again. "And it's right here in Nairobi. You probably never even heard of it. My class and I are going to Kibera."

Ajene felt weak in the knees. He hoped his children hadn't noticed how quickly he'd sat down to avoid falling.

Ajene had never been interested in Kibera or its desperate people until that fateful day when he knocked his golf ball over the wall separating the slum from the country club, the event that gave rise to his meeting Moses. Except for the day he accompanied the teachers to Moses's hut—the day he stayed too long and ended up rescuing the kids from an ominous fate—he'd never previously set foot on Kibera's parched soil. And he'd never since returned, except in nightmares.

Ajene's wealth had provided him a great deal of authority and independence. As one of Nairobi's most affluent attorneys, he always did exactly what he wanted to do—and refrained from what he didn't. One thing he never wanted to do again was go back to Kibera. And he didn't want his children going back there, either.

What in the world could the Nairobi school board be thinking, authorizing a field trip to a horrid place like that? He didn't intend to wonder for long.

The next morning, Ajene didn't send his children to school; he escorted them personally. When the young-sters asked him why, he explained that he needed to see an administrator. Only two of them could pronounce the word. None knew its definition.

"Why do you want to see an *admin-strat-er*?" Kamau asked.

"I have my reasons," the father replied.

"Is the *admin-strat-er* person a man or a woman?" Kamau asked.

"I don't know. What does it matter?" Ajene replied.

"Well, if you're going to ask if I can take a frog to school, you'd better ask a man. A woman might say no."

Ajene felt assured he'd concealed his anxiety about the field trip.

He entered the office of Ms. Efia Adala, where the preoccupied receptionist didn't look up when she asked Ajene if he had an appointment.

"Yes," he said, "with my attorney, if Ms. Adala declines to see me this morning. She can then talk to him."

The receptionist jolted to attention and hurriedly stepped into the office of an official who was, in fact, the principal at his children's school. Ajene overheard her telling Ms. Adala about the sarcastic man in the outer office.

"Good," he thought. "My rudeness won't be a surprise to her."

Ms. Adala was apparently unintimidated by Ajene. She kept him waiting for almost forty-five minutes. His impatience became frustration that converted into outright anger. The principal had no idea what awaited her.

Ajene was finally shown into the office, where he was asked if he'd like to sit down.

"Only if I can take the furniture after winning my petition to have your job," he replied.

Ms. Adala had no idea what he meant, but she knew his tone was malicious.

"Are you aware of plans for a field trip of young students into Kibera?" Ajene continued, surprised at his volume.

At that, a bolt of shock shot across Ms. Adala's face. She stumbled backward a step.

"Yes...well, not exactly. I mean, yes, I think so," she sputtered.

She was clearly disoriented. This triggered Ajene's lawyerly instinct.

"Would you like to answer that question again," he said, "more clearly this time?"

Still flustered, Ms. Adala took time to gather her wits. She'd heard enough sarcasm from this unwanted, unscheduled visitor.

"Sir, you can take a civil tone with me or find your way out. Is *that* clear?"

Ajene didn't expect Ms. Adala's steely response. He had long ago mastered the art of intimidation. He had not encountered many who could rebut his tactics.

He quickly realized it would be best not to test her further. She might call security. They might call the police. He didn't need to be arrested for disturbing the peace inside an elementary school.

Awkwardly, he apologized. But they both knew it was insincere. Knowing his remorse was disingenuous, Ms. Adala asked Ajene if he'd like to sit down. He sat while she continued standing. She didn't speak until she, too, was seated. Ajene knew her movement was intentional, an unspoken show of authority. He'd used the same behavioral language many times at the plaintiff's table inside a courtroom. For a second, he wondered if Ms. Adala had been to law school.

"Now," she said, "why did you want to see me? I gather it has to do with our planned field trip to Kibera."

So it's true, Ajene thought to himself. He shifted in his seat, surprising himself as he did. The movement no doubt alerted his adversary to his forthcoming outburst. He'd lost the element of surprise. Suddenly he felt nervous. He couldn't wait to hear whatever he might choose to say next.

"Mr. Jabari," Ms. Adala began, her voice an edgy drone. For the first time, Ajene thought she sounded like a stereotypical schoolteacher. "I have been principal of this school for six years. I have led as many annual field trips into Kibera during my tenure. I therefore estimate that approximately two hundred seven and eight year olds have seen a side of life they would not have otherwise seen. The sight for each has been a life-changing experience intended to reform conventional thinking about how the less fortunate live their lives."

Ajene wondered if she used such lofty language with the students.

"Not one child, not one chaperone, has ever remotely come close to harm during one of my trips," she continued. "Each child is accompanied by an adult, often a parent. Additionally, they're accompanied by faculty members and an armed detail from the Nairobi police department.

"Bear in mind that I don't expect young children to lead a feeding or medical mission. I'll leave that to the American missionaries. These field trips are purely for observation, sojourns intended to show children such as your daughter that not everyone enjoys such a privileged life as she.

"In other countries, school integration is achieved by mixing the races. In Nairobi, where almost all students are African, the issue is not race but economics and class discrimination.

"Your child will have a learning experience that can't be taught from a textbook or inside a classroom—not even through advanced curricula within this private school. The chance for learning far exceeds the chance for danger. Did I mention that our police patrol is armed? I think I did."

Ajene was taken aback and hoped it didn't show. He was supposed to be the skilled orator, the one who could think on his feet, constructing the most persuasive of arguments. For the moment, he was speechless.

Then he regained himself, as his ego would not stand for defeat in the arena of verbal jousting. In the space of minutes, he disarmed Ms. Adala with a summary of what had happened to his children and him inside Kibera three years ago. His recall could not have been clearer if the life-and-death drama had actually transpired that morning.

Ms. Adala heard it all, from the errant golf ball to the fiery escape. When he finished talking, Ajene heard nothing but the sound of his own heavy breathing inside the otherwise silent room. He knew why the principal didn't respond. The table had turned.

When at last she spoke, Ms. Adala struggled to form the words. Her bravado melted into heartfelt apologies.

"I had no idea," she said. "I had no idea." She kept repeating the words, as if to make them a chant.

Ajene appreciated her remorse and told her so. He accepted her apology and told her that, too. He shouldn't have. Once again, he'd been presumptuous, thinking he had bested her with his rhetoric.

He hadn't.

Ms. Adala was now more determined than ever to

take Nyah, along with dozens of other students, into Kenya's most blighted slum.

"In light of what you've just told me, I insist that Nyah needs to go more than any other student," said the educator. "You don't actually think that child will grow up without someday finding out about her mother and that she won't surmise her mom was a prostitute who died of AIDS? You don't really believe, do you, that she won't somehow find out about the rich man who set a part of Kibera on fire to camouflage his escape with three Kiberan children? Do you really think Nyah won't deduce that the man was her father and that the three youngsters were her brothers and her? Just how naive are you?"

Ajene started to reply, but suddenly he didn't have the energy. He'd spent all his adrenalin in his earlier oratory, and now he couldn't rally enough to banter further.

By nature, he was a warrior and words were his weapon. He never entered a fracas he wasn't sure he could win. He wasn't sure about this one. Rather than concede the argument—something he'd never do—he opted to say nothing at all.

Ms. Adala took that as her cue to continue talking.

"To say I appreciate the valor of what you did is a dire understatement," she resumed. "In fact, that may be the most spellbinding and selfless act I've ever heard of. If you were in the military, you'd be given a medal, and deservedly so. I mean that with all of my heart.

"Just as candidly," she said, "I tell you that you're much more heroic than wise. Your daring rescue did little to inform you about the place from which you escaped. And your lack of understanding is proof positive about the cultural chasm between privileged people such as yourself and those who struggle within Kibera.

"Mr. Jabari, your flee from Kibera, though daring, was no more than your running away from the worst Kibera has to offer. But it has another side—a brighter side.

"It's peopled by working men and women who scrape to provide for themselves while they strive to get out. You can see them each day when they stand in line to buy drinking water at a price seven times higher than you and I pay here in Nairobi. Many Kiberans work all day for a few shillings that will barely cover the cost of *one* day's drinking water. Yet, work they do, hoping against hope that they might be able to create something better for themselves by their labor."

Ajene was no longer a contestant in this contest of wills. He was a student, Ms. Adala his teacher. He hadn't listened this attentively since he'd fed on each word uttered by his law school professors.

This process seemed edifying. He wanted Ms. Adala to continue enlightening him, and the realization startled him. He couldn't believe he actually enjoyed having yielded the floor.

"Kibera has two faces," she said, in a tone that implied she was winding down. "Granted, it may be one of the most dangerous places in all of Africa after sundown. I must tell you that I've personally seen the platoon of men who come into the slum at sunrise simply to carry out those who've either died of disease or been murdered during the night. It's a sight I'll never forget—and I hope I never do. There's something significant about knowing the full range of human experience. But I would never go into Kibera at night. If I had to be there after dark, I'd make sure I was safe inside my hut long before daylight lost its glow. Anyway, that's what *I* always did."

Ajene sensed that he'd been verbally slapped.

"What?" he croaked, fearing he might know what she was *really* saying. "What do you mean, 'That's what *I* always did'?" he asked.

Ms. Adala looked at him in a way that made him feel as small as his stepson Moses. When she finally spoke, her voice was rigid and void of emotion.

"That's what I did—all of my life," she replied. "Mr. Jabari, Kibera is my true home. I grew up in Kibera."

CHAPTER THREE

Imoo Dawodu was dying, and he knew it.

American charity workers had subsidized a Kiberan clinic where a doctor had diagnosed Imoo's AIDS two years earlier. He'd been deteriorating with multiple illnesses ever since. Kibera had no shortage of epidemics—the only things needed to claim the life of a horribly malnourished, dissipated man whose immune system was weakening fast. Clinic personnel had repeatedly explained the process of how he would gradually die of AIDS.

Imoo had already seen it firsthand many times as—slowly and agonizingly—AIDS claimed the lives of many Kiberan men and women. In their final days of weakness, some would contract what American doctors called "a common cold," an uncomplicated sickness that progressed into pneumonia, from which patients never recovered. Imoo understood that AIDS doesn't kill people directly. It just makes them highly susceptible to whatever diseases might be going around.

In Kibera, such infirmities were going in all directions. Everyone was always sick. Those without AIDS recovered in time to contract something else. Those with AIDS seemed to contract everything and eventually perished.

Imoo lay inside his cardboard hut, where he felt the stickiness of mud on his naked back as his sweat absorbed into the dirt floor. This was July, the month when African nights are cooler than at any other time of year. He was nonetheless soaked and wondered what ailments were causing his fever this time.

"Why do I wonder?" he asked himself. "Dead is dead. A man can be just as dead from distemper as he can be from worms in his bowels."

He wondered if he had both.

Clinic personnel had stressed that more and more their medicines would lose their potency to help Imoo. They talked about white blood cell counts, T-cells, and things that were of no concern to him. He didn't know their big ideas and wondered why he'd want to learn them or anything else. He was going to die.

He blamed the Americans, who brought their culture and their medicine to Africa, where people continued to get sick and die from of AIDS. Imoo was sure the white folks from across the water had a cure for AIDS but were withholding it so all Africans would die. Americans would then overrun the continent, he believed, just as hostile African tribes overrun other tribes.

Imoo felt bitter toward foreigners. They treated his

starvation and sickness while they were healthy and of sound mind. To him, that made no sense. Why would prosperous people come from a place that he'd heard was halfway around the world just to give food and medicine to the feeble and dying? Why would they share and take nothing in return? He was sure they were up to an evil plot that would unfold against all Africans. But he cared no more about such ploys. He wouldn't live to see them unfold.

Living day to day had enabled him never to worry about the future. He had more immediate concerns.

His mind failing as dramatically as his body, Imoo was gripped by paranoia that food and medicine sent from across the water was actually poison intended to quicken agonizing death to those who accepted it. Maybe the missionaries had injected him with this AIDS virus. There must be someone to blame.

He had watched the Americans carefully when they came into his village before he moved north to Kibera. He saw them bring food, and he watched them inject colored liquids called *vaccinations* into African arms. To Imoo, the word rang of mystery and ill will.

But he never saw the visitors eat their own food or take their own medicine. Their intent, he was sure, was to slowly, subtly slaughter trusting Africans. They were so hungry and so sick they had no choice but to believe that foreigners were their friends. Many of the helpers actually came in the name of their noble leader, Jesus. He'd seen Jesus's picture in a few huts of other Kiberans who'd attended the Americans' meetings in Nairobi. Some had come home singing Swahili about this Jesus who died for their sins many years ago. Imoo never understood how anyone could die for anyone who came after them by more years than he could tally.

No matter. Imoo told himself that neither Jesus nor any Americans were inside his crowded hut at this late hour. Five other people lay inside the hovel, which was no larger than two or three vans, like the ones Imoo had seen many times in Nairobi when he still had strength to walk that far.

Deep in sleep, none of the others so much as stirred inside the hut. Meanwhile, Imoo couldn't stop shaking. He was cold, but he was still sweating. And his own moisture only made him colder.

"How could that be?" he asked himself.

There was no one to answer. In a short time, there would be no one forever. Try as he might, he could not stop fearing impending death. He noticed the dirt was sticking to the side of his face now. Sweat had begun to mix with his tears.

Abu-Bakr Ba was a witch doctor whose deeds belied the essence of his given name, meaning "nobility." He worshiped dark spirits that he'd been taught since boyhood would make believers stout in mind and body. And he was thoroughly convinced their magic worked, because one of his patients who'd eaten rotting bushmeat had actually recovered.

Abu-Bakr believed that the hundreds of sickly people all around him suffered of their own doing. They had not believed intensely in the good to be drawn from diabolical spirits, so the spirits had chosen to kill them. He'd absorbed that doctrine from a witch doctor before him, and someday he would pass it on to another privileged man of darkness, who would wisely yield to brooding spirits.

Abu-Bakr had tried to tell his compatriots why they were sick, that they were possessed with snakes in their bodies. He believed that, just as he believed that ghosts inhabited them. He'd chanted about the leeches within their brains.

Most would not listen to his traditional ways. The majority had forsaken the methods of the sorcerers that came before him, and had chosen the teachings of Americans who had brought the power of patented medicine. It had been that way since he was a boy.

His life as a practitioner of brooding, mysterious sorcery had been lonely, lost to medicine in see-through containers of brightly colored fluids.

Abu-Bakr had suffered his countrymen's ridicule as

they whispered and pointed fingers. He'd been called senile and a soothsayer. Only when the truly sick were truly desperate did they consent to his secret ways. By then, it was always too late.

That's how it had been for those with AIDS. They came out of desperation. Hoping against hope, they ate the roots and powders and animal entrails that Abu-Bakr ordered. But they didn't eat fast enough, and they didn't consume in bounty, he claimed. Many were too sick to swallow. He tried to help them but their fellow tribesmen had chased him away when the feeble were not healed quickly.

Such were the doings during his last night in Kegogi Village in Abu-Bakr's beloved western Kenya. The month was May and the year 2008 when several witch doctors were murdered by hostile people whose loved ones were not getting well. Others were just as angry at Abu-Bakr because their loved ones had taken his treatments and had died nonetheless. They became a furious mob and retaliated en masse against any and all witch doctors, telling them to save their own lives with their medicine or die at their hands. The male witch doctors moved quickly and were able to escape. But the old women, some who had helped teach Abu-Bakr his craft many years ago, were slain by the aggressors.

The body count was fifteen and was reported throughout Africa.

Abu-Bakr had been running for his life ever since, hiding wherever he could, and had finally arrived in Kibera—a place he'd heard was rife with sickness and suffering, like few others. Here, he would find sanctuary. He would care for the aged and weakened whose despairing final efforts to thwart death would compel them to listen to him. They would learn to believe in the power of the spirits—and see that man's medicine is no match for this power.

Abu-Bakr knew that some of Kibera's infirm would likely have AIDS. For them, the medicine of mortal man made for the slowing of the AIDS symptoms but never for its cure. Those people would invite him into their huts. Abu-Bakr would find among them at least one who was strong enough to ingest his herbal and animal tissue remedies. And that solitary soul would thrive, and he or she would tell others—and Abu-Bakr would live forever, just like the dark spirits he served. He had willed it so.

He also brought news about a miracle cure to those who suffered with AIDS. He'd been told of its power by two medicine men that had also fled Kegogi. It was touted, in fact, to be the only failsafe cure for AIDS. He would share it with one of Kibera's AIDS-stricken. Subsequently, all would see this infected one thrive—and all would hail Abu-Bakr. This, too, was part of his master plan.

But just now, he must rest. Soon enough, the sun would rise high. Heat would again return to the earth, and Abu-Bakr must then be where it was cool and dark. Sunlight robbed him from the power he felt in darkness.

He would seek shelter inside the hut of someone who was depleted of hope for healing. If that person were benevolent, he or she would let him stay the day. If that person truly wanted to live, he would let him stay until he was of sound body.

So, Abu-Bakr began his walk among countless Kiberan huts, where he was angrily turned away. One woman told him to return to the bush. Another cursed him and another heaved onto him scalding water she'd used over an open fire to soften her day's allotment of greens. Abu-Bakr ran until her screaming was out of range of hearing.

Breathing heavily, the aging witch doctor peered through cracks in a hut at a man whose eyes were cast emptily on the moist earth beside him. The sorcerer recognized the vacant gaze he'd seen all of his life. Imminent death brought the same stare to all who were dying.

"I can help you," he whispered to the listless man. "I can help you."

Imoo's eyes rose to see a face without form, obscured by the morning sunlight behind it. He wondered about the stranger's identity but felt entirely intrigued by his promise. Imoo thought he might be dreaming. Was this person an answer to his prayers? Was he a man of medicine or of superstition? He was dressed no differently than other Kiberans. He talked of helping. Could he really render the deliverance of which he spoke?

Imoo quickly decided that the visitor's methods were of no matter. The stranger couldn't hurt him, not any more than the passing of time that, for him, was limited to a few pages on a paper calendar.

Weakly raising his hand, Imoo gestured for the intruder to enter his dwelling.

"I am Abu-Bakr, a man of unseen healing spirits," Abu-Bakr said. "The spirits tell me you are dying and that only they can save you."

Imoo noticed Abu-Bakr's small beads. Then his eyes fell to the visitor's pouch. Its puffy bulge indicated that it contained secrets without shape or definition. He no longer wondered about the identity of his intruder. Imoo had not seen a witch doctor since he left the bush as a small boy.

Abu-Bakr was surprised to see Imoo rise to greet him. Earlier his posture had formed a limp bend that suggested he was weak beyond measure. The witch doctor felt silently thrilled when he saw the return of

Imoo's energy. This meant he might respond to the remedy Abu-Bakr would share.

"The spirit of mystery and unknown has led me to you," Abu-Bakr announced.

"I don't want mystery, and I don't believe in the unknown," Imoo replied without asking for a name, without giving his own. Civil ways were unnecessary toward someone he'd never seen before and would never see again, Imoo reasoned to himself.

"You've heard of men like me since you were a boy," the visitor continued.

The stranger was not one for small talk. Before Imoo could speak, the visitor spoke again.

"You are dying with the AIDS," Abu-Bakr continued. "Even those who give you drugs from across the water have told you they will not save you. This I know. And I know their medicine makes you sick, even sicker than you are."

Imoo wondered why the witch doctor was telling him things he already knew. Nevertheless, he invited Abu-Bakr to sit, pointing to a spot on the earthen floor that was dry.

His visitor had an air about him that seemed restless but self-assured. Imoo braced to hear about remedies that had probably been passed down to Abu-Bakr from remote jungles centuries ago. If nothing else, they would make for good stories—tales that might take his mind off his pain, if only for a while.

But stories and myths were not forthcoming.

"There is only one cure for the AIDS," Abu-Bakr said, his voice returning to a whisper. "Only *one* cure. Many in all of Africa are using it now. It was found a few years ago, and news of the remedy has spread from village to village to doctors like me in all tribes of every nation."

Imoo's silence bid his guest to continue.

"Your affliction came from the passing of tainted fluid that you got from a woman," Abu-Bakr said. "Only pure fluid from a pure woman will heal you. Nothing else."

"You must lie as one with a virgin. You must pass your tainted fluid to her. You will then be made well, indeed."

There, on that wet and sticky floor, Imoo felt himself reel. What had he heard? The idea of sex with a virgin as a means of healing was an outrage to all of human-kind—and to anyone's God, he felt sure. What forces of insanity and evil had entered his hut with this stranger?

His churning mind raced to another quandary—the notion that a virgin could be found in Kibera. Many women there have babies as soon as they come into womanhood, he knew, and most women are had by men long before that. Thereafter, many sell their favors for as little as a shilling. Inside Kibera, finding a virgin seemed as preposterous as the search for wealth.

Imoo wondered if Abu-Bakr knew the kind of place that Kibera was. If so, he must be senseless. *What would a senseless man know about the healing of AIDS or any other affliction?* Imoo thought to himself.

When Abu-Bakr again spoke, it was as if he'd read the dying man's mind.

"You're thinking what virgin and where, are you not?" the witch doctor said.

"It is true," Imoo replied.

"Virgins are here," Abu-Bakr continued. "But they are not yet women. They are still only children."

The sorcerer's directness no longer startled Imoo. It infuriated him. Imoo had once had children of his own. Both of them had died from diseases born of Kibera's main source of water, a creek filled with animal urine and excrement, as well as an occasional floating carcass.

Imoo's rage might have compelled him to strangle Abu-Bakr for his suggestion, if he'd had the strength. But he did not.

The sick man's aggression remained unexpressed because his burst of energy had diminished as rapidly as it had arrived. All at once, he felt too weak to stand, much less to fight.

Easing to the floor, calmer thoughts reminded him he'd not been surprised by the sorcerer's horrific prescription. He did seem to remember talk about the new AIDS cure known as the "virgin cure," espoused by old, mysterious witch doctors who haunted the wilds outside the cities adorning modern Africa. Growing calmer still, Imoo now remembered hearing Kiberan women speak of news reports, and he recalled their passing a tattered Nairobi newspaper whose pages were yellow and brittle. It presented a story they wouldn't share with the men, warning women about ignorant, desperate men who would stalk their young daughters, then rape them in a superstitious and final act to save their own lives.

Imoo certainly never thought he'd actually meet someone who recommended the crazed remedy, especially not ten miles from Nairobi, the largest city in Kenya—much less inside his own hut.

"I will return tomorrow," Abu-Bakr told Imoo. "Until then, you ponder. Ponder how you will live. The virgin will lose her childhood but not her life. She is young and doctors like me—even the American medical doctors—are coming closer each day to a cure for the AIDS. She will not be sick long enough to die. Her youth and strength will let her live for the medicine that will make her fluids pure, her body whole. But your health is gone. Take the virgin now and recover, and you both will live. Ignore her and she will live but you will die."

"I will return when the sun rises again." With that, Abu-Bakr eased from Imoo's door as quietly as he had entered.

Imoo stared at the ceiling of his hut, now dimly lit by the risen sun. He could see his hand as well as the container he and his family used to relieve themselves. A mess of *sukuma wike* (collard greens and tomatoes) was on a stool, situated there by his daughter before she had gone to her day's labor and her children had gone to the Kiberan school. With no electricity or any other source of light, everything around him appeared as a dim silhouette within the flimsy hovel.

Imoo lay back down. He could not stop thinking about the witch doctor, about his AIDS cure—the taking of a virgin—and how she might fall sick but not die. When she got older, would she not be glad she had only endured a passing sickness to extend the life of a dying man? Imoo began to talk himself into committing the unspeakable act.

Could it actually be true? How could it not? If the rumor were not trustworthy, it would not have passed from tribe to tribe until finally arriving in dark, despairing Kibera. And if it were not true, why was it published in Nairobi's newspaper? Did the story say the rumor was untrue? Imoo did not know. Kiberan women had not allowed any men to read it and wouldn't talk about it.

His mind was a frenzy, swinging wildly between desperation and hope. Was his hope just the impossible wish of a forlorn, dying man? Was he thinking rationally now, or were his thoughts merely lost in dreams?

He considered the source of the information, the promise of recovery. It had been offered by a shaman— the kind of man who trades in myths and lies. But didn't liars tell the truth at least sometimes? And did the truth care who told it? The truth was truth, regardless of the source.

Imoo was astonished at the clarity of his thinking now. He prayed to any god who would listen, whether the Sovereign one of Americans or the vile one of the witch doctor. Which, if either, had sent Abu-Bakr to his hut?

Just then, he heard conversation and footsteps outside his hut. Many strangers were passing by, talking about Kibera and the disadvantage of those who exist within it.

Coming out of his reverie into reality, he was certain he heard the chatter and laughter of children among the group. He could even tell the little boys from the little girls.

Abu-Bakr didn't enter Imoo's hut quietly. Not this time.

He stooped before bolting through the tiny door but his reluctant companion did not. She was short enough to negotiate the low passageway while standing upright. Abu-Bakr had brought Imoo a schoolgirl.

Everything became a blur.

Abu-Bakr's hand covered her mouth. He pulled tightly against her head, holding it against his sweating torso. Her screams were muffled beneath his strong, lean palm. Imoo saw blood trickling from the witch doctor's hand. He knew the child had bitten him. The veins on the back of Abu-Bakr's hand were rising as he tightened his pull of the child's head and neck against him. Her struggle was no match against her muscular captor.

"This girl is a virgin," the witch doctor exclaimed. "She has to be. Look at her fine clothes and washed face. She is not a Kiberan child. I took her from among several schoolchildren walking with elders. You must have her quickly. Soon she will be missed."

Imoo knew he wasn't dreaming now, but he certainly wished he were. To his horror, he saw a helpless child wrestling harder now against the witch doctor's muffling grip.

Imoo knew he was expected to rape her.

"This is not chance," Abu-Bakr said, straining to keep his voice down. "The spirits have sent this virgin to you. They might not send another. There is no search now for an unspoiled girl. You must take her before the elders come looking for her. They are with police. They would certainly arrest us or perhaps even kill us without trial."

Imoo felt the beating of his heart rise into his throat. He could not speak.

"Remember my teaching!" the witch doctor commanded, his voice breaking from a whisper to a low, grating rasp. "She might not catch the AIDS. But she can take medicine if she does, and there will be new medicine for her before she has time enough to die. But, you will die soon if you don't have her!"

All of this was too much too quickly for Imoo. His confused mind could not process what he'd just heard, except the parts of about the child's chance to live and the certainty that he would not.

Unless he took her.

With his hand still locking the girl against his waist, Abu-Bakr thrust his other arm around Imoo's neck. He seemed stronger to Imoo than many men his size as he pushed the girl to the earthen floor and forced Imoo on top of her.

"Prepare yourself!" the shaman ordered.

Imoo's preparation was fast. He feared the witch doctor might kill him if it wasn't. The act was over almost before it began. The child had begun to bleed and was kicking violently as Abu-Bakr pulled her from beneath the weeping Imoo.

Abu-Bakr used one powerful arm to raise the child off the ground, the other to maintain the smothering grip across her still-screaming mouth. Her teeth had broken flesh in several places on the witch doctor's hand. His blood dripped onto the dirt floor.

The schoolgirl had held her eyes tightly shut in terror the entire time. Imoo doubted whether she had even seen him as he took her virginity and scarred her for life.

"I must return her to safety, to a place she will be found," Abu-Bakr said. "I will return tomorrow. Your healing has begun. You will be void of the AIDS and well in body."

Then, as quickly as they had entered, Abu-Bakr and the schoolgirl were gone. In the space of minutes, the witch doctor had overturned the worlds of two people he hadn't known before the sun had risen yesterday.

Imoo lay on his naked back in the dirt. He felt moisture—it was warm, a pool of the little girl's freshly spilled blood.

Ravaged by guilt, he lay there for almost the entire day. Would his cure be instant or gradual? He'd forgotten to ask Abu-Bakr. Surely it would come slowly, he finally decided. He certainly wasn't feeling any better so far.

Imoo felt no better the next day or the next. His condition progressively worsened until he could no longer distinguish one day from another. That's how his life went on for weeks, until the very day he died.

CHAPTER FOUR

THE BACKFIRE OF a car bolted Ajene from today's afternoon nap. He had determined to be especially attentive to his children today, as he felt guilty for having missed Nyah's field trip.

The adoptive father wondered why he'd awakened early this morning with a feeling of foreboding so intense that he became nauseous. He'd spent most of the morning throwing up and had even asked a neighbor to drive his kids to school for him. After the youngsters departed, he continued experiencing unfocused fear, as if something was horribly wrong or would be soon. The more he worried, the sicker he became. He was sure he had become dehydrated from retching repeatedly.

Simply too sick to accompany Nyah's special outing, Ajene later beat himself up emotionally for missing it. The event had been the subject of jubilant anticipation inside the Jabari household, where Nyah had talked about nothing else for days.

"Do you think the girls in Kibera will like me, Daddy?" she had asked repeatedly. "Can I bring them home, but not all on the same night? Do you think the boys there are icky like they are at my school? Are the grownups nice like you?"

The child held no idea of the relentless poverty and squalor that awaited her during her organized pass through Kibera. Ajene had pondered and prayed, hoping the culture shock would not overwhelm his seven year old. Kiberan children cope with their living conditions because abject poverty is all they've ever known. Children who successfully live there were born there—just as Nyah had been, though she refused to remember. He reminded himself that her repression of Kiberan memories before age four was a normal thing. All of the psychologists had told him so, and they couldn't all be wrong.

Ajene had even felt his own sense of anticipation gradually mount toward today's Kiberan excursion, especially since the stormy clash he'd had with Ms. Adala. His worry about Nyah's safety was renewed, but not enough to override the logic Ms. Adala had presented: it seemed necessary for Nyah to see life's other side while her childish acceptance might help her to avoid developing the typical prejudices that most adults tend to share.

Ajene had agreed to be one of several parental chaperones and looked forward to walking beside policemen who would escort the troupe through Kenya's most desperate and dangerous slum. Seeing her dad walk beside a uniformed policeman would surely cause Nyah to think her dad was "special"—perhaps even more than America's SpongeBob.

Soon she would burst through the front door, excitedly reciting all she had seen, Ajene imagined. He anticipated her starting each sentence with, "Daddy, you should have been there when..."

Why had he gotten sick today, of all days? Why was he forced to miss the trip? He had no idea the questions would haunt him for the remainder of his life.

A ringing telephone jolted Ajene from daydreams.

He said hello to a caller who did not return the greeting. He instead identified himself as an officer with the Nairobi police department and asked if he were speaking to Ajene Jabari. Before Ajene could reply, the policeman asked if he had a daughter named Nyah.

Ajene's back hit the sofa even before he felt his knees buckle.

"Yes, I am her father," he said, instantly gripped by fear.

"Let me explain," said the invisible voice. Ajene was glad the caller had taken the lead in the conversation.

"Your daughter, Nyah, is an emergency patient at St. Demetrius Hospital," he said. "Do you know how to get there?"

Ajene's mind collapsed. He wasn't sure he could make sense of what he was hearing. A voice he had never heard had just told him his only daughter had been taken to the ER and had asked if he knew the way to the hospital.

"I...Yes, I know how...well...It's not far from...Of course, I'm coming now," the addled father replied.

"A policeman will be expecting you," said the caller. "Please identify yourself to the officer in the emergency room."

"What's the matter with Nyah?" Ajene shouted into the telephone. "Why are you calling? What's going on?"

He posed the question repeatedly but received no answer. Deafening silence followed each time.

"Please identify yourself to the officer at the hospital."

Ajene was instantly out the door, hurriedly leaving it ajar. His mind flashed on his car but he opted to run. He'd never before realized that St. Demetrius hospital was only six city blocks from his house; he counted each block while crossing intersections, needing something to do with his mind to keep from falling apart.

He'd never been so afraid, not even three years ago on that terrifying night when he'd rescued his children from what otherwise would have been their fiery graves.

Already he was telling himself he shouldn't have let Nyah go back there, even if the army had escorted her.

Ms. Adala was surrounded by school personnel and adult chaperones outside an emergency room examination stall, where the wails of patients intermittently spilled into the hall. She raised her head when Ajene entered, then instantly glanced downward, avoiding eye contact. Ajene recognized a few parents, all of whom were murmuring under their breaths or not speaking at all. No one approached him. When Ajene tried to engage them, every eye gazed toward the floor.

"What is so interesting about the floor?" he shouted to no one and to everyone. "Will somebody tell me what's going on? Where's Nyah?"

The chaperones were themselves like children, shifting their feet and waiting on someone else to speak up. No one said a word. For all Ajene knew, she was missing. But that made no sense. If she were missing, he'd have been summoned to the police department, not to a hospital.

He'd had enough. He'd probably been here for thirty seconds—what seemed like an eternity in his frenzied state of mind. A door bore a sign reading "Hospital Personnel Only." He started through it.

Ajene had forgotten about reporting to a waiting policeman, but the officer hadn't forgotten him. He was detained at the private entrance.

"Are you Ajene Jabari?" the policeman inquired.

"Yes," the father replied, trying to brush past the imposing lawman.

The official put a firm hand on Ajene's shoulder and let his other palm fall to his nightstick. Ajene realized what the cop meant to communicate by that gesture.

"May I see some identification?" he asked. Ajene wondered how someone could be obsessed with identification at such a time. The issue here wasn't his paperwork but his daughter's welfare.

"In your wallet," the policeman offered, seeing that Ajene was totally disoriented.

He looked at Ajene's driver's license, then looked at his face, and once more at the license.

"Well, you are who you say you are," the officer said dryly.

The policeman's entire demeanor instantly transformed from menacing to compassion. The glaring transition was simultaneously reassuring and frightening to the father, who still had no idea why he was called to the hospital ER.

"Your daughter has been assaulted," the officer said.

"Assaulted?" Ajene replied. "Is she hurt? Did you catch the guy?"

"Well...she's been raped," said the policeman. "The doctors will tell us soon how badly she is hurt."

Ajene experienced an explosion of anger and grief

that defied his self-control. He was somehow stricken mute and could feel the movement of lips that produced no sound. He felt himself make a fist and started to raise it against the officer, the bearer of this horrific news. Instead, he exploded into uncontrollable sobbing, but not because he was sad. His were tears of fury.

Ms. Adala was the first to approach his side. He was then surrounded by parents and teachers and others attempting words of comfort. One woman actually dropped to her knees and began to pray aloud.

"Nyah somehow wandered from the group," said Ms. Adala.

"She was there one second and gone the next. We stopped, and all the policemen with us ran from hut to hut. She was nowhere to be seen."

"How did you find her?" Ajene shouted.

"Out of nowhere she stepped from between the huts near our group," the supervisor answered. "She was bleeding on her face and within her pants. She was screaming and stepping here and there."

Ms. Adala's voice simply trailed into quiet, as if it had evaporated. She was clearly fighting for self-control herself when Ajene broke her silence.

"What happened then?" he bellowed and saw people beyond his circle look his way.

"The policemen asked Nyah who had hurt her," Ms. Adala continued. "But the child could not answer. She could only stammer and scream. The police officers tried to comfort her but she withdrew instantly from their attempts to touch her. She ran to the arms of the women. That's how we guessed what had happened to your precious little one."

"I want to see her now!" Ajene yelled loudly, his voice breaking from volume. He began to curse and threatened everyone within earshot with a lawsuit, including the police officer who was trying to escort him to Nyah.

"I will not take you to see your child until you settle down," said the officer.

Ajene threw himself into forced composure for Nyah, not for the people he was upsetting around him. Someone gave him a handkerchief and a woman chaperone ran a comb through his hair.

As he was being taken to his daughter, guilt and a sense of failure possessed him, but not as much as the fear he felt when he finally saw his little girl.

CHAPTER FIVE

NYAH HADN'T SPOKEN since Ajene had brought her home from the hospital nine days ago. Depleted, he reiterated the prognosis of doctors who'd said Nyah would ease from her earlier hysteria into post-traumatic stress. Then she would likely lapse into depression—quite possibly a catatonic state of mind. The predictions proved to be as accurate as a map.

When admitted to the hospital, Nyah was heavily sedated as doctors procured a vaginal swab that might identify her rapist. She then underwent two abdominal operations to repair her torn vagina. She howled in humiliation as she was examined regularly to change her bandages and to be sure infection had not invaded her stitches.

Each examination triggered a total loss of emotional control. Doctors eventually had to bind her with restraints, fearing she would try to flee her bed, despite the presence of Ajene, her dad. Nyah had no response to him, even laying with her face toward the opposing wall. She neither spoke nor made eye contact with him.

Nurses said Nyah would want nothing to do with any man for weeks, maybe months. Ajene had read that child rape victims typically reject all males after their attack. He thought he could live with that. But health workers didn't know the rest of the story behind Ajene's fear: that Nyah would disdain him because he had sanctioned her trip into Kibera. Based on the assurance of Ms. Adala, Ajene had promised his daughter she'd be safe, that she'd undergo a life-improving experience. He prayed the naïve and terrified child would realize he never foresaw anything like this. It had taken three years to build the trust between his children and him. Ajene knew it could all be erased by this overwhelming tragedy.

He was confident that his little girl did not understand why doctors and nurses wearing masks and headwear continued daily to probe the sensitive place where she'd been hurt.

Nurses advised Ajene to leave the room during each examination, as his child would be embarrassed around her dad about what had happened to her *down there.* He had earlier made himself absent during the first round of testing intended to identify Nyah's rapist, an ordeal he strongly challenged. He knew he was overly protective, but the idea of medically invading Nyah in hopes of catching a phantom infuriated Ajene.

Nairobi police rarely entered Kibera, much less

responded to its crime, simply because they feared for their lives within the lawless slum. How could they ever identify or locate a suspect? Kiberans were practically stacked on top of each other inside virtually identical mud and cardboard shanties.

How could a fugitive be accurately described? Hundreds of thousands of men in Kibera shared the same traits—malnourished, desperate, unwashed, impoverished, and starving.

The policemen with Nyah on that horrible day were officially off duty and had been paid by the private school board to accompany the youngsters. The cops were joined by perhaps twenty parents. The entire troupe proved powerless. Why hadn't they done *something* to protect his child?

Ajene intended to sue them all—individually and in class action. He was suddenly glad that he'd spent his adult life as a trial lawyer. He would personally participate in the litigation. Ajene vowed to make it his life's quest to garner a judgment that would take everything these people had, knowing none of it would replace what his child had lost.

At that moment, he didn't care that his intentions were selfish and unfair. Vengeance, not fairness, was his incentive. He would begin the legal work just as soon as his daughter was well enough to appear as a witness.

So what if doctors had taken a fluid sample from his daughter's attacker? It was unlikely the suspect's DNA would be on file with Nairobi police. If it were, how could he be arrested? It's not as if the daily-changing population in Kibera ever posted forwarding addresses.

To make matters worse, a policeman who had questioned Nyah minutes after she arrived at the ER had complained about her fleeting recall.

"She said she saw no one, as her eyes were covered by someone's hand," he had written in his report. "She was so afraid that she kept her eyes closed. She knows only that she was taken to a hut with a dirt floor. That is every hut in Kibera."

"What do you expect from a terrified child?" Ajene had yelled at the officer.

Their dialogue ended in stalemate. Given the policeman's attitude, Ajene could only assume that Nyah's case was closed as soon as it had been opened.

He and his daughter must learn to live with the outrage, even as the man who committed the crime remained free.

Yet Ajene could not understand what kind of maniacal pervert would forcibly rape a primary school girl. He had no idea that the ravishing of virgins was epidemic in Kibera and other impoverished parts of Africa due to superstition among HIV-positive, AIDS-beset men who believed sex with a virgin would save their lives.

"As more and more virgins are taken, the desperate have to resort to younger and younger females," an investigator had explained. "Your little girl was with a group of prosperous people from Nairobi. She was bathed and dressed well, her garments pressed. It was clear she was a virgin. That's why she was raped. The rapist might lose his self-respect, but he thinks that's a small price compared to losing his life. In his eyes, he really has nothing to lose if he rapes her. If it doesn't heal him, he would have died anyway. That's how he thinks."

Ajene didn't care about sick men and their impending deaths from AIDS. He cared about his daughter's life and her will to live it. He wished he could find the man who'd stolen that desire, the man who had left her unable to look at any man, including her own father.

Ajene's violent fantasies made him wonder just how civilized he actually was. Given the chance, he knew he'd kill the assailant—and do it as brutally as his seething, angry mind could contrive.

Month in and month out, it continued—Nyah's withdrawal from life into the cocoon of her room, where lights were always extinguished and blinds were always closed. Each day was like the last, a hollow exercise in listless living by a child who ate only when food was left at her door and who showered much too frequently, scrubbing her skin until most of a bar of soap had depleted. Each time she cleansed, she insisted her brothers be locked inside their rooms, as she didn't want them to accidentally see her undressed.

Her suspicion toward males only increased with time.

Doctors had warned Ajene that Nyah would exhibit abnormal behavior rooted largely in exaggerated self-protection. They hadn't told him it would last this long.

His child's depression was now beyond measure. The doctors recommended hospitalization, but to no avail. The mere mention of returning to the care of scary men in white coats and facemasks always sent Nyah's emotions spinning over the edge.

Her Kiberan attacker had violently penetrated her on one terrible occasion. The men in uniforms had done it many times, and had done it while other men and women in starch had looked at her. Those in uniform had also used thread to sew inside her and heavy and shiny things made of metal to later remove the threads. Always, they painted her tummy with medicine, colors that would not wash away for days.

Desperate to comfort her, Ajene decided to ask some of Nyah's schoolmates to visit her, thinking the warmth of their friendship might draw his daughter from her shell. She screamed like a panther at the suggestion, saying only, "They will look at me and know what has happened down there."

Ajene's efforts toward restoring Nyah's mental health were taking their toll on his own. His sense of guilt was unbearable. Neither he nor medical personnel could come up with any idea that served to restore the demeanor of the happy little girl whose current misery he'd helped orchestrate.

As a last resort, he engaged the services of two female psychologists who regularly came to Nyah's bedside. The diagnosis was always the same—"severe and acute psychological and emotional despondency."

"Time eventually heals all wounds," one of them told Ajene. "Only time will heal this."

At the tender age of seven, Nyah remained locked in the vise-like grip of a nervous breakdown. She wasn't dying. But she seemed to wish she could.

Months passed. Until the time of the rape, no one, male or female, had ever raised a hand to her. Now whenever she closed her eyes the sweaty and filthy hands of the witch doctor were again mashing her face, closing her nostrils, and covering her mouth. In her mind, she relived her terrifying inability to breathe. She often felt like she was suffocating. Ajene could say nothing to convince her otherwise.

Through her bedroom door, Ajene often heard Nyah

gasping for air when there was no reason not to breathe normally. She forcibly breathed just because she could, fearing an imaginary time when she could not. Sometimes she momentarily passed out from hyperventilation.

When silence told Ajene she'd at last fallen asleep, he'd slowly peek inside her room, only to see her coiled in a fetal position with her hands cupped around her lower pelvis, the best she could do to ensure that no one would ever hurt her there again.

Then there came a breakthrough of a sort, but only for a while.

Nyah let her father sit on her bed. It was the closest he had been since the night before the attack. The two stared silently into each other's faces for what seemed like hours. It didn't matter. He was communicating with his little girl via unspoken words, eye to eye. He remained locked in that loving gaze until Nyah finally turned away.

One night, having given no other indication that she might be ready to come out of her shell, Nyah finally spoke.

In a voice weak from not speaking for so long, Nyah asked her father if everyone in Kibera was as poor as the people she'd seen. She wondered, she said, because she had not gotten to see it all.

"A policeman took me away quickly with another policeman inside a car that made a loud, whining sound," she said.

Ajene told his child that all the people in Kibera were, in fact, as poor as those she'd seen.

"But Kibera sits beside the place where you play golf, Daddy," she replied. "You play on the big lawn of the president. I saw your place to play golf when I looked up from Kibera."

Ajene felt ashamed of the contrast between his life of privilege and the poverty of the Kiberans.

"That's right. I do play there," said Ajene, wondering how to explain class distinction to a sick child.

"Daddy," his daughter continued, "do you think the people in Kibera do mean things because they're hungry and poor and the people where you play golf are nice because they are not?"

Ajene had no idea how respond. It didn't matter. Nyah continued expressing her innocent curiosity.

"You know what you should do, Daddy?"

"No, sweetheart, what should I do?"

"You should take the children at Kibera to the nice place where you play golf," she said. "They might get to have nice things there like you do, and when they get big, maybe they won't be mean grownups like the men who were mean to me."

Ajene was astounded. Through her natural inclinations, his little girl had assimilated the fundamentals of sharing wealth and alleviating social ills. He felt proud to the point of tears. Though seriously ill, Nyah wasn't thinking of herself but of children who'd never known a comfortable life like hers.

Ajene had never told Nyah anything about the real world. She didn't seem to remember that she was born in Kibera, nor anything about her experience there during her first four years of life. As her protector, he had preferred that she would never have to remember— that her only childhood memories might be those of enjoying spacious housing, private schools, clean sheets, fashionable clothes, America's SpongeBob, and the best he could provide. Ajene had long ago decided that his best was better than anything that anyone else could do for his children.

He also hadn't told Nyah that her assailant had done more than physically hurt her and leave her forever terrified. The unknown man had made her a part of the pandemic.

Soon after her rape, his only daughter had been diagnosed HIV-positive. More recently, it had become full-blown AIDS.

Nyah's health seemed on a slippery slope, sliding faster and faster.

Her depleted immune system finally failed and surrendered her to tuberculosis. Ajene could not accept this horrific fate befalling his innocent baby girl, just as he could not accept the vehement incident that ignited it all on that cursed field trip into Kibera.

Why tuberculosis? She had obviously never smoked a cigarette or inhaled secondhand smoke. There were no air-polluting factories near their pricey residential neighborhood.

Then he recalled something Moses had said about Nyah's Kiberan mother, who had died of an AIDS-induced infirmity before that fiery night when Ajene rescued the child and her brothers. Moses had often told him how his mother's breathing was labored. Was this tuberculosis?

In Africa, AIDS beckons tuberculosis, pneumonia, anemia, renal failure, meningitis, diarrhea, and other diseases that would be treatable if were not for AIDS. Tuberculosis alone kills 80 percent of AIDS sufferers in Uganda and throughout South Africa. It's also a primary killer of AIDS sufferers throughout Kenya.

It seemed that fate was asking too much of Ajene to see how AIDS could invade and destroy the pristine world in which he was rearing his children. Surely no God of heaven or Earth would allow the unspeakable pain to continue for long.

That has to be true! Ajene thought. *God is love. So where is His love now?*

In his more rational moments, Ajene knew he wasn't the first father to pose this question to a God he couldn't see regarding a tragedy he couldn't understand. He knew that if an answer were to come, it wouldn't come in this world. Maybe an explanation would avail itself in the afterlife, in heaven.

Right now, he didn't want to go to heaven—or anywhere else where God might reside. He was furious with God, whomever or whatever God might be. If God could save Nyah's life and did not, then He wasn't a savior at all, Ajene decided. Any God that would let her die was a monster, and the distraught father wanted no part of such a person, spirit, or whatever He was.

None of this troubled thinking helped his precious Nyah. He'd been warned that she was likely to die an agonizing death in her own bed within Ajene's protective sanctuary.

The tuberculosis had begun when Nyah inexplicably developed spasms and was taken against her will to a clinic. She would allow only women to attend her—and only those women willing to shed their medical frocks, of which Nyah was afraid. Each attendant wore a mask with a smiling face drawn on it, hoping this might calm the child's fears. Nyah thought the women looked silly;

especially the jolly nurse who'd sketched teeth onto her encrypted grin.

For a second that day, Ajene thought he saw Nyah smile. He feared it might be the last time.

Her TB had been diagnosed by a respiratory specialist and confirmed by another who treated tuberculars exclusively.

"Your daughter would not have succumbed to this, were it not for the AIDS," the doctor said. "Given her age, good nutrition, and environmental factors, her immune system would have fought it off. But I must tell you now that your little girl is going to be one more casualty in the failing war against HIV. We are a continent ravaged by torturous deaths from the silent killer."

Very poetic, but so what? Ajene thought to himself. *Most of the others who are dying are impoverished and had little chance to live anyhow. I saved Nyah from a slum and all of those indignities years ago. I didn't raise my clean, beautiful, healthy little girl to be a casualty in anyone's war against disease.*

"How could a one-time encounter with one foul creature end the beautiful life of someone so pure?" he said. Ajene was talking aloud, not sure anyone was listening and not caring if they were.

And so it came, the beginning of the end for his precious Nyah. Desperate, the hapless father retained three shifts of bedside nurses administering the most effective sedatives and anesthetics available in Kenya's pharmacies. He conducted a one-man crusade, hoping somehow to activate a miracle that might save her life. He made promises, trying to bargain with the God in whom he still wasn't sure he believed. He told the hospital board of directors that he would bequeath his estate to their administration if they could prevent Nyah's death or at least significantly postpone it.

To a person, the hospital staff told the distraught father that his little girl was going to die. Do what he would, he could not undo death's tightening grip.

"Soon she'll suffer no more," a doctor said. If the remark was intended as consolation, it failed miserably.

Ajene began to believe the dire prognosis when he entered Nyah's room to find her peeking from beneath her blankets, pulled snugly against her nose.

"Daddy, I'm so cold," she whispered.

He turned off the central air-conditioner and activated the heat. He and his two sons sweated thereafter, and no one complained.

Within days, Nyah's skin became flushed. Her eyes glistened, taking on a vacant and sickening trance.

As time moved on at a snail's pace, her breathing became inconsistent and then noisily labored. But the worst was yet to come.

Six hellish months passed. Perspiring from the sustained heat of his furnace, Ajene bent over his child and noticed his sweat falling into the tears on her face—a mask of confusion, posing a question about the pain that consumed her.

"Daddy, I wasn't mean," she whispered, barely audible. "Why is this happening to me? Did we forget to give me an aspirin? Remember when you gave me aspirin for a toothache?"

Ajene was undone by her innocence. His baby girl actually thought all of this agony might go away with the swallowing of an over-the-counter tablet. So he gave her a couple of aspirin. They weren't going to hurt. And if Nyah thought they helped, he'd give her as many as the directions on the bottle allowed.

Nyah's throat clutched when she was unable to swallow the dry pills. Her spasms were then uncontrollable.

Ajene paid a doctor four times his regular fee to make a house call and to explain why the TB seemed to be progressing so rapidly. The physician said he could offer no concrete explanation, although he could tender a possibility.

"Before the AIDS and tuberculosis, your daughter was extremely healthy," he explained. "Her formerly strong body is actually accelerating the TB's progression. The disease is feeding off her stamina. In a curious and figurative way, it's as if it's thriving off her earlier vitality."

"Is anything even remotely fair about this prolonged process of dying?" Ajene asked the physician.

The doctor began a response, but the depleted father cut him off. He'd heard enough about medicine from too many people, not one of whom was making his child well.

"I don't care about your theories," Ajene screamed. "Just do something to relieve her pain. Do it now!"

"Her pain is now stronger than my medicine," the doctor replied. "My presence here gives you only false hope. I must now assist the child the best way I can. I must leave. Please know I am so sorry."

The room was swallowed by silence so pronounced that Ajene could hear the brushing of the doctor's shoes against the carpet as he stepped from Nyah's room. Seconds later, he heard the quiet closing of his front door and the doctor's fading footsteps, until they were no more. The medical profession had run out of answers. Nyah was running out of life.

Ajene erupted into uncontrollable sobbing, something he vowed he'd never do in front of Nyah. Almost instantly, Moses and Kamau burst into the room, fearing their beloved sister had passed. Seeing their hysterical father, they too began to weep.

Nyah could only stare at the flowing tears. The charade was over, and she suddenly knew it.

"Daddy, I'm dying, aren't I?"

Ajene fought to form the words, any words that might resemble a reply. But he didn't need to speak.

Sharp pains shot through Nyah's body, and she began to contort. Her vomiting, which had been still all day, suddenly reappeard along with diarrhea. Ajene and his boys eyed their beloved Nyah. Still convulsing, she cast pleading eyes to her daddy, begging silently for help. Helpless, Ajene knew well the full angst of the matter: there was nothing that could be done. He and his sons would relive this nightmarish moment countless times before death finally took her.

From that day on, neither father nor brothers ever left Nyah, except to go to the toilet or to bring her soft puddings. Eventually a nurse stopped the pudding, insisting the milky substance would induce even more vomiting. This might result in strangulation. Shortly thereafter, Nyah could hold nothing down—not even water.

"The dehydration will soon take her," the nurse said

lovingly, placing one of her hands on Ajene, another on Kamau. "She won't die vomiting. This way is best."

Totally spent in mind and body, Ajene could offer not a whimper of dissent.

And so it was. Nyah's struggle to breathe became an endless series of desperate gasps, a sound to which Ajene and family grew morbidly accustomed.

At one fateful sunrise, Ajene lumbered to his feet once again from another night's fitful sleeping on the carpet beside Nyah's bed. He could feel the rug's imprint on his burning face.

Looking down at Nyah, he saw that her eyes were open and empty, fixed and staring at the ceiling. Even in death, they seemed puzzled as to what had happened to her and why.

Ajene wondered once more if there really was a heaven.

With tears streaking his unwashed skin, he looked upward, believing that his baby must surely be looking down at him. Her confusion, like her pain, was finally gone forever.

A little girl who had been rescued from Kibera at age four was dead because her father let her return at age seven. That's the way Ajene saw it. He knew he would be haunted by guilt until the finale of his own days.

The weight of it all was like a boulder resting on his chest. Were it not for his two sons, he might have chosen to join Nyah in eternal sleep.

Ajene's respiration was an endless stream of sighs. He'd grown wearier since Nyah's passing two days ago. When she was hanging by a thread, he had lived to prevent her passing, hoping for a miracle that never came. Now she was gone, and each moment was a void he couldn't fill, not with thoughts or with deeds.

The funeral had been planned. The phone had stopped ringing with endless inquiries from friends and associates. Even that nosey reporter had stopped badgering him about writing the story of a Nairobi child who'd died of AIDS after being raped. For the first time in months, Ajene found himself absolutely idle.

Repeatedly, he heard a dark, accusing voice reminding him that he'd let Nyah attend that Kiberan field trip against his better judgment. The voice said he was foolish to have succumbed to the persuasiveness of a school administrator who promised Nyah's safety.

"Why did you give in to her arguments?" the voice taunted. "The field trip was not for the children; it was for her professional résumé. She didn't really care about Nyah's education, just as you didn't care about her welfare."

"Silence!" Ajene shouted.

"Who are you talking to?" Moses called from the next room.

Ajene didn't answer.

He'd heard members of Nairobi's Christian community talk about recognizing the still and small voice of Jesus Christ. If they could really hear His voice, the voice Ajene was hearing must surely be the devil's.

People would later tell Ajene that the funeral flowers were beautiful and how natural Nyah had looked inside her coffin. Why, he wondered silently, did people reduce his life's greatest pain to small talk?

He remembered only parts of the minister's remarks from the funeral. He offered very little comfort, very little insight, very little to ponder. It seemed as if the tired old pastor simply repeated the hackneyed sound bites for the bereaved.

"Precious in the sight of the Lord is the death of his saints," the minister had droned.

So what? Ajene had wondered. *This isn't about anybody's Lord. This is about my daughter. Did the Lord ever lose a daughter?*

As if he were reading Ajene's mind, the speaker continued about God identifying with the suffering, as He'd lost His only Son to crucifixion.

Well, after all, He's God, Ajene thought bitterly. *If He's all-powerful and omniscient, I guess He planned it that way. But why did His plan include the taking of my daughter? I don't know if His Son really died for me, but I know I didn't ask Him to. Where was His compassionate Son when my baby was being raped? When she died?*

What am I doing? Ajene suddenly thought. *I'm arguing with the preacher who's delivering my daughter's eulogy.*

Anger, not grief, was his predominant emotion. He knew it, and he didn't care.

"Look at you," the unwanted voice whispered. "You're furious when you're supposed to be brokenhearted. Some father you are."

Was this the voice of his conscience? Ajene had never known it to be so outright ferocious.

Who had sanctioned this minister anyhow? Ajene asked, again probing himself. Nairobi was filled with clergymen who believed in God but didn't advocate that "personal relationship with Jesus" thing the American missionaries tended to preach.

"Steal away, steal away, steal away to Jesus," the choir was softly singing. Ajene had been so lost in thought

73

that he hadn't noticed when they shuffled into formation behind the preacher.

"Steal away, steal away home. I ain't got long to stay here."

The father was jolted into the moment by a bolt of recognition. He remembered this melodious dirge from his undergraduate study in world humanities. The song harkened to a time when flesh traders had been abducting slaves from Africa, transporting them to a life of toil and ignominy in the West:

> Now He didn' give you dat baby, by no hundred thousan' mile!
>
> He just think you need some sunshine an' He lend it for a while.[2]

Ajene had forgotten that the hymn gave voice to the pain of a brokenhearted couple at the funeral of their baby.

Did whomever planned this service think these words would be consoling?

"That person was about as bright as the one who'd planned a student field trip into Kibera," Ajene fumed, intentionally returning to the safety of his bitterness.

But the bedeviling voice in his mind began to torture him anew.

"Nyah was a hapless victim of the desperation so

prevalent among poor people in the world. Those who took her to Kibera took her in hopes that she might see injustice and feel motivated to work for change. Instead, fate determined that she'd never have the chance. But you? What's your excuse? What are you going to do about the continuing desperation that prompts the violence your daughter suffered? You don't know? You don't care? You're right on both counts. And so, your daughter died in vain."

The preacher's words interrupted the speech in Ajene's head, saying that no one knows the ways of the Lord. To Ajene's surprise, the minister touched on the evil that hides in the hearts of men and throughout the world. Ajene sat upright, hoping to hear what might explain this evil, why God allows it to exist. Ajene imagined, based on his own experience, that hell was not some mysterious place removed and underground, but an invisible blaze all around him right here on earth.

"Suffering and agony beset all of us every day," the preacher continued. Ajene realized he could no longer tune out the minister, whose words began to resonate within him.

"Emotional pain is the result of sin, the disobedience to God's law. When man sins, he acts out evil, and he eventually suffers. But sometimes others suffer, too.

Some are inside his family, some are outside, and some are in families yet to be born."

The preacher referred to the sin of Adam in the Garden of Eden, claiming he responded unduly to the influence of Eve and partook of the fruit that God had declared forbidden. The effect of that original sin had passed through to the next generation—their son, Cain, had killed his brother, Abel. The preacher asserted that sin was still manifesting itself amid mankind, citing the shaman who had likely influenced a desperate man to violate little Nyah. The consequences of Adam's original sin had echoed across centuries, now claiming the life of Ajene's innocent little girl.

"And to the loss of life's meaning for her father," Ajene added silently.

He wished the preacher would stop talking or change the subject. He had wanted to hear his child eulogized, not a lecture on the nature of malice in the world.

He already knew about evil all too well.

This preacher can't help me solve the mystery of why Nyah had to die, Ajene surmised. Once again he was able to tune out the speaker's words as he continued to drone.

There was no logical answer as to why Nyah's innocence had been stolen and her life taken by fatal violence. Search though he may, Ajene would never find peace of mind. This matter was beyond the reach of human reason, absolutely lost to it. Resolution and peace would be found only in finding faith, he surmised.

There was no other option.

Christ's forgiveness of him, Ajene's forgiveness of those who perpetrated the outrage on his daughter—was there something to the shopworn message the preacher had dedicated his life to convey?

Ajene knew he had plenty of sin in need of forgiving. Chief among them right then was his anger toward God and Christ.

Feeling powerless and exhausted of other choices, Ajene was desperate enough to take the leap of faith, approaching God through Christ—but not today.

In spite of himself, he had heard and understood much of the preacher's message. He wanted to mull it over, let it all soak in. Tomorrow, perhaps, he might accept it all as truth.

"But not right now," he said to himself. "Not right now."

Ajene's pain only deepened over time.

His boys had gone back to school after a week of grieving, and he resented that their bereavement was coming and going on their personal schedules. His own never let up.

A psychologist had counseled the boys on three occasions. He had insisted to Ajene that they needed school, its surroundings, and all that was familiar. The environment and routine would not immediately heal their emotional wounds, the doctor explained, but it would help put an end to the bleeding.

Moses led Kamau to class, repeatedly asking him if other boys could tell that he'd been crying. Kamau said no, so Moses made him promise not to tell that he had been.

Their morning departures were the entry to Ajene's solitude. The empty house was disconcertingly alive with memories. The silence was deafening.

Ajene walked vacant hallways and hollow rooms where his wailing seemed to echo. He went to the bathroom to throw up, mostly dry heaving. His unexplained nausea had kept him from keeping anything down, even liquids. He thought about calling a doctor, but was too depressed to dial a telephone. He'd have to work his way up to such a daunting task. Perhaps he'd start by finding a fresh box of facial tissue. It was a beginning.

The grief counselor had warned Ajene about post-traumatic stress and had said that the most intense suffering would come in about six weeks. Ajene's had arrived ahead of schedule.

He stood above Nyah's bed, weeping onto fresh

sheets that someone had put on the mattress. He didn't know who; so many people had come and gone during the days between her death and the funeral.

"Where are they now?" Ajene asked aloud.

The counselor had warned that he might sink into a well of self-pity. Ajene hoped he'd drown.

He surprised himself when, inexplicably, he darted to the family's clothes hamper, frantically searching for Nyah's soiled sheets—the last thing she'd touched before dying. The linens weren't among the household's dirty laundry. Little wonder. Caked with vomit and excrement as they were, someone had wisely thrown them away.

The last physical remnant of his daughter had been discarded like unwanted refuse. Dare he look inside his outdoor waste receptacle? Did he want to see the flies swarming, or other vermin that feed on human waste? Was he insane for wanting a part of her, any part, no matter how foul?

His mind was a whirl of rampant irrationality, for sure. Insanity? Let it come. Ajene didn't care about anything.

Why, why, why had he let her go into Kibera? The question was tired and unanswerable, but it would not go away. Nyah's teacher had insisted the trip would be good for her, alerting her to the human problems of poverty, ignorance, and the depravity that so often results from them.

"So she learned of these things!" he shouted. "So what? How much good did it do her? She's dead!"

"But Ajene, *you* are alive." The voice in his head was back.

He hadn't heard that small, brutally honest voice since the funeral. This time, there was no mistaking the truth in the words, the authority of the tone.

Ajene could do nothing to bring his daughter back to life. But he could himself take action on what she—what they both—had learned from her tragedy in Kibera. He was alive. And he could do much to save other lives. He was here to do the very things Nyah might have grown up to do after her life-changing walk through Kibera.

His whirling psyche raced to what he imagined may have been Nyah's trauma at seeing the sick and dying, all suffering in the shadow of Kenya's placid playground for adults. Even his innocent little girl had acknowledged the glaring unfairness of a handful of elites having so much prosperity while a million Kiberans had nothing.

Memories were now invading his mind. Once again they whisked him back to the night he'd rescued Nyah and her brothers from Kibera after their mother's death from AIDS. Ajene's little girl had forgotten or had totally suppressed it all. Kibera would forever remain lost in human tragedy because no one empowered to usher change cared enough to do so.

The grief counselor had warned Ajene that his memory would be spotty. Ajene had forgotten about the meddlesome reporter who'd so insensitively interrogated him after Nyah's death. He therefore wasn't prepared for what he was about to see.

These days the monotonous drone of the television provided his only company. He left it playing nonstop to provide distraction from the stranglehold of his loneliness.

And then they resounded, words whose impact rivaled a clap of thunder: "AIDS resulting from rape has slain the daughter of a wealthy Nairobi lawyer, according to this morning's edition of the *Nairobi Herald*," the newscaster said. "More after these messages."

Who else could this refer to but Nyah? He didn't need to wait until after commercial messages to fetch the morning newspaper. He bolted out the front door.

Ajene ransacked the disorderly pile of unread papers cast aside the front steps, furiously opening each issue.

Quickly enough he spied the screaming headline: "Rape Brings Death by AIDS to Nairobi Child."

A six-column story filled most of the cover, then jumped to an inside page. The reporter had procured a picture of little Nyah taken from her elementary school yearbook. Another large photo depicted the festering conditions inside Kibera. In all of his years in Nairobi, Ajene had never seen a photo of Kibera on the newspaper's front page. If ever featured, such pictures were small and buried deeply inside editions beside a short blurb about an unsolved murder committed by ghastly means.

This story about Nyah portrayed her as an unwitting martyr, a wealthy child whose death focused attention on the latest insanity spawned by the AIDS pandemic—the idea that men might deliver themselves from the ravages of the disease by raping virgins, even young children.

The text went on to talk about the evolving Africa, how its transformation still left much to be desired toward eliminating the ravages of poverty, ignorance, and desperation. It traced the arrival of witch doctors from faraway villages earlier in the year, citing them as the source of current madness.

On the editorial page, an opinion keyed to Nyah's story challenged Kenyans to find new ways to address the old-world superstition still so prevalent that it had actually claimed the life of a child from an affluent suburb.

"The AIDS pandemic among the poor has now penetrated the world of the wealthy," the editorial began. "The ignorant, superstitious sacrifice of this delicate girl should alert us to the deaths of countless others who are forfeited every night and day inside Kibera and other African slums. What is next, the sacrifice of newborns?

"Those of us who are materially blessed are ultimately the ones with Nyah's blood on our hands if we don't overhaul our thinking. Until AIDS is cured, we must find a way to eradicate the poverty, stupidity, and myths surrounding it. The disease is killing not only its victims but also now the victims of the victims.

"In the words of Edmund Burke, 'All that is required for evil to prevail is for good men to do nothing.'"

Ajene stopped reading. He could no longer see the newsprint through his tears.

Maybe his little girl hadn't died in vain. In fact, in a sense, she was more alive than ever in terms of what she was inspiring in others. It was as if she'd merely gotten a promotion from earth to heaven and relocated there to continue living on, to even greater effect. The funeral preacher had suggested as much.

Nyah's news story assumed a life of its own. It was picked up by a newswire first in London, then throughout the world. Ajene's telephone rang for days with inquiries from journalists across the continent and across the water.

The published words of reporters he'd never met touched Ajene's heart repeatedly. Their writing posed questions about a responsible society's previous unconcern regarding AIDS and its agony that haunted him and filled him with a gnawing sense of guilt.

How dare he think he held a monopoly on misery? What about the untold millions of Africans, many of whom had lost mothers, fathers, sons, and daughters, just as he had lost Nyah? No newspaper had reported *their* stories. What about the loved ones who'd suffered their agonizing fate without benefit of the anesthetics that he'd procured for Nyah? Had his wealth and privilege bred a blind eye to the suffering of those who did not enjoy his bounty of resources? Those people lived without even the common safeguards, such as education and contraception, that Ajene had taken for granted since he was a child.

He had been obsessed with crying for himself. Who would cry for the children who were yet to die? Who would speak for the people who could not speak for themselves?

CHAPTER SIX

JENE WAS ONCE again immersed in an emotional cocoon while teetering on the brink of sleep. He was dreaming, but not so deeply that he didn't recognize the sound of a bell. He felt a vague sense of déjà vu, recalling this same scenario when Nyah was alive.

There was another ring, and still another before Ajene was effectively jostled from slumber, taking him back to the suffocating grief that sleep had helped him to temporarily escape. He was no longer a refugee from pain. It had returned to slap him awake.

Ajene recognized the next bell. It was the intrusive tone of his door chime. When had he experienced this before? Oh, yes—it was when his children, all three of them, had come home from school and caught him dozing on the couch.

He staggered unsteadily to his front door and opened it to face a squadron of men, all golfers from the Regal Kenyan Golf Course. He had played with each of them, and his law practice had even represented a few. Ajene couldn't avoid looking over their heads at the parked convoy of imported luxury cars. He was sure the neighbors would think an auto auction was underway, but the brokenhearted father didn't care what anyone thought.

"We read the newspaper story about Nyah," said Mwenye Dube, one of the group's youngest members. Ajene assumed Mwenye was the unofficial spokesman for the gathering, as he was emotionally closer to the young man than he was to the others. The twenty-something had recently graduated from law school and was serving a probationary term at Ajene's firm. He had personally selected him.

Ajene had noticed Mwenye's intensity when he had lectured at his undergraduate school. When the floor had been opened to questions, Mwenye had spoken first and more often than any of the other students. The seasoned lawyer had eventually taken the dedicated student under his wing and offered him the job shortly after his law school graduation.

Little Nyah had formed a crush on Mwenye and had asked her dad if he thought the young lawyer might want to marry her. Ajene had explained that men his age don't ask little girls to wed. Nyah seemed fine with the response.

"I know you are a grown up and can't ask if I'd like to be your wife," she told Mwenye.

"That's right," he responded. "I can't ask a pretty little girl like you."

"OK," Nyah had responded, "you don't have to ask. I'll marry you anyhow."

The child did not understand why her dad and the object of her affection were laughing, and her disappointment turned into tears. Both men quickly restrained themselves and mustered their best explanations as to why a six year old couldn't marry an "old" man. Their most convincing argument was that "old men" did not enjoy American television's *Hannah Montana*. If Nyah married Mwenye, she would have to give up Hannah for life, they warned.

That sacrifice was more than she wanted to make.

"I hope I don't hurt your feelings," she offered as an apology to the young barrister. Mwenye assured her he'd live with the disappointment.

Ajene was surprised at the vividness of his recollection. He suddenly realized that the golfers at his door had waited patiently as he'd become lost in his daydream of his departed child. Their compassion touched him, and he knew it showed. So what? He'd gotten past the point of suppressing his emotions the first time he'd visited Nyah in the hospital, the day of her rape.

Mwenye resumed speaking, jolting Ajene back into the present moment.

"Everyone here is stricken with sorrow because your precious one died of the AIDS forced upon her. We regret that one of the last things she understood was the injustice between our privileged world and the desperation of Kibera's. That's a large issue for we who are grown. Your little girl certainly should not have felt her mind invaded by topical issues. She should have been free to enjoy her childhood."

Rubbing sleep and bewilderment from his eyes, Ajene wondered why Mwenye had led these men to tell him what he already knew—what everybody knew—about outrageous class arrogance among those at the Regal Kenyan and about those on the other side of its Kiberan wall, where fighting for life is a losing battle.

"Ajene," Mwenye continued, "Nyah became an unwilling martyr. But she didn't die in vain. The newspaper story about her has brought much attention to AIDS orphans. If your little girl had the courage to enter Kibera, we should have the courage to make people aware that children there are left without their people because of AIDS. Innocent children! Some are born with the AIDS themselves! For these young ones, unfairness abounds."

Ajene felt impatient. Mwenye had said nothing that wasn't common knowledge. Were these men actually adopting the cause of AIDS babies and orphans? Did the high-profile rape and death of his child finally shake these wealthy people from complacency? Had her demise actually served as a clarion call to draw attention to the disease that is killing a continent? Ajene's curiosity began to rise along with his annoyance.

"Why are you here, on this day, in front of my house?" he snapped with no attempt to moderate the challenge in his inflection. The men, all at a loss for words, looked blankly at one another.

"Talk!" someone said, nudging Mwenye.

"We have an idea for a charity event benefiting the fight against AIDS," the lawyer-in-training continued.

"Many here watch reruns of American golf tournaments when they're shown on African television. Our idea is to invite one or two famous American golfers to play a benefit tournament with players from the African PGA. We will use the American embassy to establish a dialogue and arrange the event."

Everyone in the entourage was of like mind and lobbied for Ajene to let them name the event "The Nyah Jabari Memorial Golf Classic." Their cajoling was unnecessary. Ajene had been ready to consent to the project the instant he'd heard the idea.

And so it began—Mwenye and two dozen prominent men in quest of a charity tournament on Nairobi's lush course adjacent to its infamous slum. Nothing like it had ever been done, nor even considered, by Nairobi's disconnected social elites.

Because a prominent child had died, a few of the rich were stepping up to help the countless poor. If miracles came with numbers, Ajene knew he'd witnessed the first.

A tournament date was set, and planning intensified for an unprecedented event.

International media interest was intense, "as if the Olympics were going to be staged in Kenya," commented one Nairobi columnist. Ajene would eventually concur; the statement seemed to be not much of an exaggeration, as reporters from outside Africa converged on Nairobi. A major American sports magazine sent writers to Nairobi to create articles revealing the dichotomy within Africa's social structure, about how the wealthy, without precedent, were finally breaking their tradition of self-involvement and actually looking at misery all around.

"Compassion was finally ignited," penned a journalist, "after the daughter of a wealthy Nairobi lawyer fell victim to the merciless savagery that the poor female children of Africa face every day."

America's newswire services hummed with articles and commentary on the pending change in old-world economic discrimination. One paper quipped that the probability of members at an aristocratic African country club helping their destitute neighbors had seemed about as likely as America's Republican Party holding a fundraiser for Democrats.

"We would have wagered that capitalism and

socialism would entwine before Kenya's wealthy would lift a finger to help the sick and starving," said a wire service editorial. "Little Nyah was a heroine unaware and is clearly Africa's answer to America's definition of *hero.* "

The broadcast media relayed these stories over the airwaves, producing stories that were channeled to the African bureaus of the cable news syndicate and aired coast to coast in the United States, as well as throughout Europe.

"David is going to fight the Goliath of poverty," proclaimed one newscaster.

Mwenye and other tournament organizers were besieged by sports agents representing professional golfers who wanted to participate. The fledgling tournament turned into a "see and be seen" affair for those players wanting to raise their international profiles.

Champions from America's US Open, its Masters Tournament, and the British Open jumped at the chance to play in the first-ever competition of its kind. Some had previously come to Kibera on missions to distribute food. Now, those same athletes were going to play golf to benefit the desperate region.

For decades, managers of the Regal Kenyan had shown nothing but indifference toward their sick and starving neighbors. The golf tournament finally sparked their enthusiasm—though not so much for compassion as for capitalism. The televised promotional value of the upcoming contest would draw legions of wealthy visitors to the members-only country club. Tourists visiting Nairobi on safari might now want to play its history-making fairways. A one-day pass could be sold at an outrageous fee, and new revenue to the Regal Kenyan coffers might be beyond projection.

That all this might continue to be about helping the helpless was just too much to hope, it seemed to Ajene, shaking his head sadly. Sometimes he wondered if he ought to share such thoughts publically rather than keep them to himself.

The well-worn sheen on the fabric of Ajene's tuxedo indicated he'd spent too much of his adult life inside Nairobi's aristocratic power structure. He had always attended the right balls, graced the proper parties, and indulged the politically correct charities.

He was nonetheless astonished at the gigantic turnout of wealthy attendees—Africa's beautiful people—who rallied on the day of the charter tournament to benefit AIDS orphans in Kibera. The president of Kenya was on hand, and because he was, presidents from other African countries joined him in his royal box.

Ajene meandered persistently through the teeming gathering in search of Mwenye. Finally, he found the young man; he resembled a human pack mule, holding scorecards and tournament fliers in both hands, under his arms, and even between his teeth.

"I can't thank you enough for putting this event together," Ajene told Mwenye, who could only grunt in response because of papers clenched in his jaw. Ajene promptly removed the obstructions.

"Thank you," Mwenye said, gasping slightly. "Now I can't give out these fliers. They bear the prints of my bicuspids."

Ajene was tempted to laugh, but amusement was lost to the thankfulness that was overtaking him.

"You know, I adopted Nyah and her two brothers, who are somewhere around here avoiding their father," Ajene said. "They became my instant family. You've been like an older brother to them, and I've discouraged that. I was afraid of the conflict of interest, since you work for my firm."

"I could tell," replied Mwenye. "And I did not—"

"Never mind," Ajene said, cutting him off. "There are plenty of lawyers in Africa, and not enough older brothers," he said. "Mwenye, you are welcome inside my home to be with my two remaining children at any time. I would want them to grow up to be like you, with your work ethic and competence and personal character."

Both men were embarrassed, and Ajene searched for something to say that might ease the discomfort.

"If you were not so old," he told Mwenye, "I would adopt you, too. As things are, you might someday run my law firm. When that time comes, I beg you not to fire me."

The quip was the best Ajene could do without preparation, but it worked. Both men laughed, and both knew that each cared deeply for the other. They broke eye contact and resumed the task at hand, separately scanning the assembly of AIDS children who were the trendy cause of the day.

One socialite said the AIDS orphans tournament would do more to raise her profile than Nairobi's celebrated marathons for Kenya's long-distance runners. She told a reporter she simply had "no idea what to wear to this worthy gala, intended to keep unwashed people from catching that dreadful AIDS thing."

Ajene reeled when told that gate receipts approached one million American dollars, most of it tendered by walking spectators whose galleries numbered almost thirty thousand. He decided he was being unduly cynical. What ultimately mattered was the calling of attention, as well as revenue, to the AIDS crisis. If a spectacle attended by the insincere was needed to do that, then so be it, he concluded.

Nevertheless, he couldn't help feeling suspicious.

How much of today's proceeds would actually benefit AIDS orphans, and how much would remain with the country club?

But, he didn't want to think about that now, not during the final minutes of a glorious day prompted by the end of his daughter's life. He wished she could be here to see the festivities, especially her name, emblazoned across a banner over the entrance to the Regal Kenyan Golf Course.

Then, for an instant, Ajene wondered if he were dreaming. Scores of tiny faces were peeping over the infamous wall between Kibera and the golf course. Each countenance was present for perhaps a minute and then dropped out of sight so another could appear. The children of Kibera were taking turns sitting on each other's shoulders to catch a glimpse of the event that was officially being staged for them. The line of little faces went up and down like human pistons.

The playful resourcefulness of the orphans raised derisive glances among those who had paid dearly for tickets, clothes, and placement inside the best spectator boxes, as well as admission to the preferable walking galleries. A United States reporter likened the affair to America's Kentucky Derby, where wealthy women dress to be spectacular and hope that the horse race doesn't draw attention away from their designer ensembles.

"Have these people forgotten that the poor and dirty

children who spawn their ridicule are the ones they're paying dearly to save?" Ajene wondered out loud to himself.

He ambled closer to the reserved seating grandstands, where he overheard talk that no one was trying to muffle.

"Who told those urchins they could spoil our day by watching?" asked a woman.

"Oh my, the ambience is being blemished by their dirty little faces," said another.

"Why must we tolerate the behavior of the uncouth?" mumbled still another.

The remarks increased in number and in volume. So-called polite society was manifesting the worst of impolite commentary. Soon an audible groan floated across the haughty gathering each time a meager new face appeared on the Kiberan side of the fairway.

The loudspeaker announcer who had introduced each golfer was asked by a tournament official to tell the youngsters to stop peering over the fence. He made the request and his words prompted soft applause among the snobbish spectators. But the plea was made to no avail. Kiberan children had never previously seen pomp and circumstance, not to mention thousands of people in a single cluster. Their naïve curiosity could not be stifled.

Ajene instantly thought of the words of Marie Antoinette, who was told the masses were starving and had not a bite of bread. "Let them eat cake," she replied, with no idea about the ignorance of her remark as it pertained to the plight of the penniless. Ajene knew that many of the rich women at the day's festivities might just as likely tell Kiberan children to go play with their toys—which, of course, none of them owned.

Someone approached the announcer with a note, and he read it over the public address system.

"Tournament officials have requested all police and security personnel to form a line against the Kiberan wall in order to prevent the children from distracting our esteemed patrons," he said.

Ajene was sure the announcer had no idea how ignorant he'd just sounded. It was undisputedly clear now that Kibera's starving children and AIDS orphans were no more than a passing reason for the wealthy to frolic. Tournament sponsors might share some of their money, but none of their concern, not even their glances toward those who needed their help. The mere sight of the beneficiaries was spoiling the glee of the charity patrons.

As ordered, police and other uniformed personnel were soon staring eye to eye with teary youngsters, telling them they could not look over the wall to watch the tournament or the people who attended. Children were ordered to keep their feet on the ground.

"You'll never be a part of this world," one officer told the children. "No reason for you to look at it."

Ajene suddenly remembered how Nyah had looked at the opulent course from inside Kibera. She was an impressionable child who was changed by the sight, as she had repeatedly told her daddy until the day she died.

The rich women surrounding Ajene had seen only a small part of Kibera, and they too were changed—for the worse. They were annoyed by the mere sight of the suffering with which others had to live. Each seemed to seek opportunities to look away.

The police action cast a pall over the previously jubilant festivities. Many Americans and Europeans, in a spontaneous and disorganized show of protest, abandoned the grandstands and galleries for the parking lot and their rented cars.

Jack Holloway, a ranking American golfer, had been set to tee off on the first hole when the inflammatory announcement had been made. He had paused to watch the authorities respond. Disgusted by the treatment of poor children, Holloway simply walked away from the competition, asking where he needed to go to scratch his entry.

Television reporters searching for a human-interest angle instantly knew they had one and focused their zoom lenses on security personnel scolding Kiberan children on the other side of the wall. One policeman was videotaped as he placed his hand atop a child's head and pushed it downward out of sight.

Holloway virtually sprinted toward the television camera and, without invitation, stepped in front of its lens. "We golfers were trying to do something nice for poor children who are orphans of AIDS," he lamented. "But some of these people in the galleries have turned this benefit match into a party for themselves. The kids aren't even invited! Well, they can keep my entry fee— provided they don't spend it on manicures or designer watches—but I'm going home! If anyone feels the same, they should follow me to the fastest way out of this place!"

"I'm with Holloway!" shouted a furious spectator, his words leaking into the television microphone. Instantly, other fans and players shouted their discontent. Thus, a charity founded on compassion became a mass exodus of irate participants and spectators. Some of the African wealthy who hadn't wanted the Kiberan children to see the tournament also stormed away. They knew that appearing on camera at an event where policemen were restraining deprived children was definitely not the kind of public relations they'd been hoping for.

The spirit of merriment was squashed. The sea of spectators moved in waves to the parking lot, making their exit. The Regal Kenyan Golf Course had unwittingly shown its true colors, the darkest hues of class discrimination. There was no distinction between the races, just between the *haves* and *have-nots*.

Walking to his car, Ajene felt heartsick and wanted to be alone. He was not pleased when a tattered old woman wearing identification as a day laborer approached him with a child in tow. He wondered what she wanted, but not enough to converse. He simply wanted to get away as quickly as possible, away from people with swollen portfolios and empty hearts.

CHAPTER SEVEN

JENE HAD NOT seen Moses and Kamau all day, as they had opted to play with other children rather than watch the golf match. Each thought the game was boring. Ajene's original plan was to pick them up at a nearby playing field on his way home. But, having heard the announcer's caustic pronouncement as it floated from the loudspeaker to their playground, Moses and Kamau had decided to meet him at the car.

Just as the boys were walking up, the old woman spoke. "You are the kind man who used to be jaded," she said without introducing herself.

"What?" Ajene asked, instantly wishing he hadn't responded.

"You used to be jaded, like the people who attended this event. But then you adopted Moses and Kamau and kept them after the passing of Nyah," said the withered woman, her frail voice fading.

"How do you know that?" Ajene replied, curious but fighting his impatience.

"I am ShuShu Wangal," the woman said. "I am the mother to SiSi, the dead mother of Moses, Kamau, and

Nyah. SiSi came to me in my village after giving birth to a female baby. Her name is Tobi. SiSi begged me to take her because she knew she was dying; she knew she could not care for a newborn baby. How could I say no? No one knew of Tobi's existence, not even Nyah or her brothers."

Ajene felt his legs weaken beneath the load of emotion at hearing this astonishing, bewildering news.

"What are you telling me?" he asked.

"I'm saying your family has another orphan of AIDS, one you did not know, not until this day. I have raised her 'til now. You have papers about my daughter and the certificates of the births of her other children. Here is the paper about the birth of Tobi. Your sons now have a sister again, and you again have a daughter, if you want her."

Ajene let his weight fall against his car door that was still ajar.

"I speak the truth," said ShuShu. "I came to work here for this one day for a few shillings because I knew you would be present at this happy time for Nyah."

As a lawyer, Ajene had always prided himself in being good at reading people. Eyeing her deeply and carefully, he felt certain the woman's claim was genuine.

Ajene eyed his boys, then the toddler who'd been presented to him as their sister. The physical resemblance was striking to a degree that surpassed coincidence.

He reached to pick up Tobi, but she cried and clung to her grandmother. It was then that Ajene noticed the old woman's tears. He knew she had brought her granddaughter to him hoping he would take her, adopt her, as he had her brothers and late sister. Obviously she wanted what was best for the child. That she loved her dearly was clear. And her wanting what was economically best for the child did not lessen the pain of letting her go. Ajene pretended not to notice that she was weeping.

"ShuShu," Ajene said, "I once left Kibera with three children, who later became my own. Because of a fire, I didn't have time to think about it. Today, there is no fire. Nonetheless, I feel no need to think about it."

She didn't understand what he was talking about.

"Never mind," Ajene said. "I invite you to come with all of your grandchildren to my house. I could use a grandmother's love and care for my family, whose numbers seem to expand each time I leave Nairobi's city limits."

His attempt at humor also fell short of the old woman's understanding.

"I will come to your house and care for this family," said the old woman. "How long might I stay?"

"Well, let's have a long talk about that when we get

home," Ajene said, "a very long talk. We'll probably need to talk about it for the rest of your life."

Ajene felt as if he'd undergone a daylong ride on an emotional roller coaster. The height of his jubilation had fallen to despair when the children the charity event was intended to benefit were treated so maliciously and the tournament fell apart. A few golfers had actually asked for the return of their entry fee and that their names be eliminated from the players' roster.

"I agreed to play so I could help needy children, not see them humiliated by a bunch of rich people who attempted to make this a high society soirée," Mwenye told the entry chairperson.

His words evoked a smattering of applause from three professional golfers behind him.

Excepting the chance encounter with his late daughter's grandmother, the entire event had been a washout, Ajene dejectedly concluded. It had been a sweet idea turned bitter. Africa's debut pro-am was intended to benefit AIDS orphans while simultaneously highlighting a pandemic that was killing an entire continent, but getting people to donate money to the cause had been easier than getting them to acknowledge the crisis. It had been easy for the rich to open their wallets, but not their eyes, much less their hearts.

The destitute but overjoyed children of Kibera had made an irrevocable mistake by excitedly jumping up and down to show their gratitude to benefactors on the other side of the lush golf course. Innocent and naïve, the youngsters thought the wealthy spectators cared about them—not just the fashionable tournament. The children's biggest error was to look at folks who didn't want to look back at them.

Ajene was situating ShuShu and Tobi into his car when Mwenye appeared from nowhere. The older man turned from the boisterous children to face the younger man who, more than anyone else, had orchestrated the day's charity event.

Perhaps he wants to talk about gate receipts, Ajene imagined. "Can't this wait until I see him at the office? Now is not a good time," he said.

Realizing his debt of gratitude, Ajene nonetheless decided to indulge Mwenye. But as soon as his eyes fell on Mwenye, his heart broke for the young man who'd worked so hard to do a good thing that had gone awry.

"Mwenye," Ajene said, before hearing whatever his friend had on his mind. "Words fail to express my gratitude for the history you made today. It had its rough spots, like any other outing that's new. But next year's tournament will go more smoothly. As far as the controversy with the Kiberan kids wanting to view the play, well, maybe next year we can build bleachers reserved for those boys and girls. It will all work out—and only because you are the one man who, in time, will raise an untold amount of money to save an untold amount of lives. You'll be a part of my life forever. Thank you, Mwenye. Thank you."

The junior lawyer and amateur golfer looked nervously at the ground and then spoke in soft tones that Ajene strained to hear.

"Do you remember when we talked about a possible conflict-of-interest regarding my participation in the tournament I had organized?" Mwenye said.

"Yes," Ajene replied, thinking the question had long ago been moot.

"Well, there is a conflict-of-interest here," Mwenye said. "I promoted this tournament to raise funds, hoping to ease the plight of children who were orphaned after their parents died from AIDS. I also wanted to allocate some of today's proceeds for research to eliminate AIDS from Africa and the planet. In doing so, I was indirectly trying to enhance my own welfare, to feather my own nest."

"I'm not sure I know what you're talking—" Ajene interjected.

"I have AIDS!" Mwenye blurted. "I have AIDS."

Even the noisy children inside Ajene's idling car seemed to fall silent. Feeling himself reel, the older man stared into the moisture welling in Mwenye's pleading eyes. Like any trial lawyer, Ajene made his living with words. If his fortune had depended on his speaking at that instant, he'd have lost everything. His mind could find no words. Sensing Ajene's bewilderment, Mwenye knew his heart was breaking anew. It was he who spoke next, simply to relieve the merciless silence.

"I had worked late one night at the office," Mwenye said. "I was gathering evidence for the director of prosecutions to bring the man who raped little Nyah to trial. We were going to surprise you with an arrest and the application of justice. But the suspect died in his Kiberan hut only minutes before we entered it. I was the first to see the dead body of the man who induced Nyah's slow death.

"I was wrenched with crestfallen pain," Mwenye continued. "I'd never felt such misery, as I so wanted to please you and impress the other lawyers in our firm. If I could have brought Nyah's rapist to justice, I knew I would have your appreciation—and the other lawyers' respect—for the duration of my career. But it was not to be. The death that claimed the rapist in seconds ended my long-range plans forever."

Questions arose in Ajene's mind. Still, he did not want to interrupt the pensive confession that was clearly addressing Mwenye's pain.

"Ajene, I am a solitary man," Mwenye said. "I have

no children, no siblings. The pain of missing the arrest, after weeks of tireless research, was mine alone to bear. I left the office and went to a tavern. I did not plan to drink so much; I did not plan to meet a woman. But with amazing accuracy she empathized, describing just how dejected I felt. She wanted to be of comfort to me she said again and again.

"I went with her to a room where money, not my comfort, was what she preferred," Mwenye continued. "By then, I could not stop. I opened my wallet and proceeded.

"The next day, I wondered why she had not required my use of protection. Only then did I worry about why she didn't fear infection. It seemed likely that she was already infected, and this proved to be true. All too quickly, I derived HIV. Too quickly again, my virus became AIDS.

"In trying to avenge the death of your little girl—and to ensure the future success of my legal career—I have given myself a death sentence. I will soon resign from the firm and focus on making my remaining days as comfortable as possible."

As suddenly as it had begun, Mwenye's report was over. Just as abruptly, Ajene realized, a young and promising life would soon be finished as well.

Nyah's death was caused by AIDS. The golf tournament and inherent controversy were instigated by AIDS.

The approach of ShuShu and her needy granddaughter was the result of AIDS. Now, the pending death of this promising young man was yet another tragedy owing to the ravages of AIDS.

Instantly, Ajene realized that AIDS went far beyond those who physically bore its torments and agonizing death. It was also devastating the lives of the healthy, such as himself, as nothing else ever had.

Feeling overwhelmed, the senior lawyer and adoptive parent wondered if he'd taken on too much. And yet here was more responsibility he felt bound to absorb. How could he care for Moses and his brother, in addition to a newfound sister and her grandmother, as well as Mwenye, whose intention had been to help everyone?

How could he nurture all of these people? The question in his heart at that moment, though, was, How could he not?

"Sit inside my car. Spend the night at my house," Ajene urged Mwenye.

And so ended a day of chaos and compassion, a day intended to be a blessing that ultimately found Ajene focused on a singularly noble, dying man and his new extended family.

Of course, the press would magnify the tournament mistakes, focusing on the sensational for a public all too ready to believe the worst. No matter, though, not now—not for Ajene. He had more than enough love in his heart and more than enough needs to fill for those he'd taken on.

As Ajene pulled into his driveway, he silently vowed to somehow devise a way to help each of them. He, himself, had plenty of time. He could not say as much for some of his passengers. Their lives, like the engine in his car, were simply idling. And like that engine, their lives would simply stop.

Epilogue

Though the story you have just read is fictional, the life-changing drama it reveals is not. Death by AIDS is a way of life in Africa.

The African AIDS epidemic has claimed the lives of so many. The latest victims are virgin girls, such as Nyah, whom you read about here. An untold number of female children have died of AIDS, contracted from rape by AIDS-infected men who wrongly believed that sex with a virgin would save their own lives from the ravages of the disease.

A United Nations report released on February 1, 2008, revealed the youngest survivor of rape in Kenya to be a one year old.[3] Pre-adolescent and teenage girls are fast becoming the largest group of AIDS sufferers in Africa. Children who die en masse often rest in mass graves. In parts of Africa, particularly the southern regions, they can't be buried fast enough. Bodies decompose in overrun mortuaries. Piles of corpses literally crush the faces of those at the bottom.

If you would like to help, you can by getting food, clothing, and medicine to children who might not otherwise have a chance at life. Many youngsters, especially babies, can be saved from AIDS if given proper medicine soon after detection of HIV in their systems. Feed The Children uses your donations to supply life-sustaining medicine and nutritional staples to children in Africa and around the world.

Please visit our Web site, www.feedthechildren.org, to see which of our many humanitarian efforts you would like to address.

For the children,

—LARRY JONES

FOUNDER AND PRESIDENT, FEED THE CHILDREN

NOTES

1.   Sarah Spencer Chapman, "From Stroud to Kibera: An Osteopath's Journey," *BBC Online*, accessed at http://www. bbc.co.uk/gloucestershire/content/articles/2008/09/03/kibera_feature.shtml on August 14, 2009.

2.   Will Carleton, editor, *City Legends* (Harper and Brothers, 1889), 125, accessed at http://books.google.com/books?id=0Z4sAAAAYAAJ&pg=PA125&lpg=PA125&dq=he+didn'+give+you+dat+baby+by+a+hunred+thousan+mile+he+just+think+you+need+some+sunshine&source=bl&ots=Vw3Q65PQVm&sig=ZTEBqleaF2cPoIVWWyZGTIz9h0k&hl=en&ei=XmCFSuW2OcO_tgfm79yvCg&sa=X&oi=book_result&ct=result&resnum=4#v=onepage&q=&f=false on August 14, 2009.

3.   Lisa Schlein, "Rape in Kenya Used as a Weapon in Political Unrest," *Voice of America*, accessed at http://www. voanews.com/english/archive/2008-02/2008-02-01-voa35.cfm on August 11, 2009.

I Lost My Ball and Found My Life

★★★★

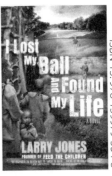

Golfer Ajene Jabari's life is far removed from the hopelessness and depravity of Kibera, one of the most violent slums in Africa. With one swing of a golf club, his privileges life crosses paths with that of Moses, a Kiberan boy who is fascinated by Ajene's golf ball. Ajene is surprised by the difference between the child's giving spirit compared to his own selfishness. While pursuing the source of the boy's happiness, Ajene finds himself trapped in Kibera's life-threatening hostility. Will he choose compassion or self-preservation? His daring decision will change two lives forever.